DIMIDIUM

Dimidium

JENIFER CRENSHAW

Hope Press

Copyright © 2023 by Jenifer Crenshaw

All rights reserved. No part of this book may be reproduced in any manner whatsoever without written permission except in the case of brief quotations embodied in critical articles and reviews.

First Printing, 2024

Love is the oldest of the Gods. You know that nagging feeling...that pull at your stomach reminding you that you're... not completely whole.... somehow unfinished.... like there is a black hole inside you? That feeling that makes you look up at the moon or out at the ocean and experience a twinge of sadness as you wonder to yourself, "Is this really all there is?". Somehow, knowing, that if united with the other part of your soul you would be empowered by a force of love so immense you could grow to unimaginable heights and tear the fabric of the universe apart? Yes... that feeling...

CHAPTER 1

YEAR: 1841

It seemed like the edge of the world. He wished it were. That way he could just step off, plunge into the darkness, as soon as she was gone, and forget his pain. His eyes took in the colorless hell before him. The gray ocean reflecting gray skies above. No sun, no light, no hope. The cold, Scottish wind clawed at him, it's screams matching the pitch of those in his head. He let his gaze fall back down on her. She was the only light, the only warmth here. Her blood felt almost hot as it fought its way through his fingers. He pressed down harder on her wound as she lay in his arms, knowing full well he would not be able to stop her life from leaving her. Overwhelmed, he shook his head, as if trying to shake the nightmare away. He felt the agony driving him to the precipice of madness.

"I can't do this again," he managed to choke out, "I don't want to do this...... I can't.... every time..." he seemed to be arguing with himself.

She stared up at him, her head cradled in his

arm. She let her hand close over his, now wet with her blood. *He's so beautiful*, she thought to herself, *always so beautiful*. But she couldn't recall the last time she saw his eyes without pain. Full of love, intensity, and lust, of course, but always, always pain. Her heart swelled and broke at the same time. She had never known what it was like not to yearn for him, feeling him with her at every moment, as though they breathed as one. How could she say goodbye now? How could she let him go? How could she go on? She took in his face, his eyes, that torture. Mustering all the strength she had left to keep her tears at bay, she reached up and touched his cheek.

"I understand," she said.

"I'm sorry. I'm sorry.." he kept repeating, shaking his head again, "I can't..."

"Shh. I understand," she said again, weaker this time. "You're my Eternity, you'll always be, even at the end." She dropped her hand to his again, her palm facing up. "Take my hand."

He looked at it, torn, broken. He would have to let go of her wound to take it. He would lose her faster and he couldn't bare it. His grip around her tightened and his eyes clenched shut, but he released her wound and grasped her hand.

"Say it," she whispered. Her blood was flowing freely now and the cold was becoming more intense. He said nothing, just held onto her, shaking. "You don't... have much time," she pressed, "if this is what...you truly... want....you must say it."

He sobbed, shaking more violently now. She could no longer hold her tears back either, she hadn't the strength. The words that escaped from his mouth were of a tone she had never heard, yet knew in her very soul. A quiet plea filled with centuries of despair, grief, and love.

"Release me," he begged. It was a knife, and its frozen blade pierced her heart, her veins taking the shattered fragments to every part of her body. She had lost him. Forever. Struggling for breath, she blinked away her tears to see his face better and their eyes locked. She would do anything to take away the agony she saw there. Even this.

"Ego...dimittis...te...amare... I love you." She took one last breath and his face blurred from view. The last thing she heard as she drifted away was a howl of merciless anguish carried around her by the screaming wind.

CHAPTER 2

Sadal pulled his coat tighter around him as he walked down the Rue de Glatigny, gliding around those in his path. A gust of wind accosted him and his hand shot upward instinctively, grabbing at the brim of his hat. *What a miserable day*, he thought. The cobblestone street was just beginning to dry after the morning rain; but from the look of the sky, it wouldn't be dry for long. He leaned into his walk, wanting to get there and back before the storm hit.

Through his peripheral, he caught sight of the child eyeballing him, and he closed his coat tighter. As expected, the child jumped into action and slammed into him then muttered a quick, "excuse moi." Sadal stopped and turned. Even though the boy faced away from him, he knew there to be a look of disappointment on his face, not having achieved his goal. Sadal had to give it to the little rascal, his pick pocketing skills had actually improved over the years, but he'd been targeted more times than he could count at this point and even successfully relieved of his coin on a few occasions so he'd had a special pocket sewn into all of this coats, a hiding place not even quick little hands could get to. "Garçon," he called after the boy. The child stopped and turned back, fully expecting to be scolded even though he hadn't gotten to steal anything. Instead, he saw Sadal holding a large coin out to him. Clearly hesitant, he approached Sadal and extended his own hand. "Mange quelque chose," Sadal said softly, offering a small nod when the boy looked up at him then continuing on his way.

Rounding a corner, Sadal came out onto a larger road, stopping quickly as a carriage crossed in front of him. He'd always enjoyed this particular part of the walk. It seemed less congested, clean, almost pleasant. Not today, of course. He felt ill at ease. And it wasn't just the weather. His thoughts turned to her, as they usually did. He'd been so hopeful when he'd arrived in this city. They had tried, many times, to find a way around this wretched curse. To designate a place to meet. Yet, somehow, every time, the memory of that place remained out of reach. Like that word that is on the tip of your tongue, but you can't quite find it. Eventually they'd surrendered to their fate, wandering beneath the stars, a constant reminder of inexplicable love and unbearable pain.

Sadal pushed on the door to the chime of a bell and stepped into the welcome warmth of his favorite building. The room was vast and bright. On one side were floor-to-ceiling windows and the other three walls were lined with books. Four gentlemen stood within the giant, circular counter in the center of the room, which lay beneath a circular opening in the ceiling, allowing a view of the two floors above. Every inch of every shelf was filled with books. Groups of fashionable ladies in bright coats and matching bonnets gaggled together, gossiping and laughing, or discussing the latest Lord Byron. Closing the door gently behind him, Sadal started up the staircase to his left to the second floor. No need for a catalogue, he knew exactly which section he was headed for.

The isles were kept dust free and, aside from the windows, which today didn't provide much assistance, they were well lit with lines of brass chandeliers, adorned with acanthus leaves, hanging from the ornately molded ceiling. His footsteps made little-to-no noise on the patterned, red carpeting and he found himself in a relatively empty part of the library. An older gentleman sat at a table, leaning inward and holding a book dangerously close to the candle, silently mouthing the words as he read. He was so engrossed that he didn't even spare a glance up when Sadal whisked past him and down the last isle. Skimming past Karl Baedeker and John Murray, he found the Cook & Son handbooks and an atlas. It was time for him to plan his next trip, hoping against hope to find her. He was just about to make his way out when he stopped. Pain slammed into him, and he had to grab onto the bookshelf for support. Within a few seconds it subsided to an ache in his chest, the same one he'd felt so many times. "Shera," he said, removing his hat and wiping away the bead of sweat that had formed on his brow. As always, he felt a ping of jealousy followed by sadness... then acceptance. He took a deep breath, replaced his hat, then set to his task with a newfound determination.

CHAPTER 3

Porri's eyes wandered to the Citadel, barely able to see it through the haze. Ordinarily, the limestone would sparkle slightly in the sunlight. Evidently, not today. Everything had taken on a gray hue, different shades. And the water looked almost black. A small boat carrying a couple of soldiers in bright red jackets slowly made its way across the Rideau Canal, their faint voices carried back to her on the mist. There were less cargo ships as well. On an average day the canal would be buzzing with ships full of flour, meat or lumber. She liked watching it, liked the activity. It quieted her mind for a while. She spent many days here, just gazing at the boats .... people .... ripples on the water. A whisper of hope in her heart as she examined the faces of the travelers.

Sighing, she continued along the road. Clutching her parasol in her right hand and hugging the bag that hung on her left arm closer, she quickened her pace. It would be night soon. The city wasn't particularly dangerous, but a woman walking alone too far from populated areas was always a magnet for trouble. And while she didn't worry about the trouble so much as the inevitable questions afterward, she'd rather avoid the whole ordeal.

Passing Queen Street, she heard the familiar sound of shouting and hammer on rock. The explosion last year had destroyed so many buildings it was hard to imagine they could ever rebuild, but here they were, erecting a new Kingston out of limestone and dreams. *Hopefully they'll find a better way to store the gunpowder this time.*

Offering a smile to an approaching couple, the gentleman's hand touched the tip of his hat as he nodded and said, "Good evening." The woman on his arm smiled but eyed her judgmentally beneath her bright yellow parasol. Porri couldn't help but laugh in her head. Walking alone and with a closed parasol, the world may as well be coming to an end. The fact that there wasn't a ray of sun to be seen was beside the point.

"Good evening," she returned, forcing herself to retain the smile until they'd reached the other side of her. Another block brought her to Princess Street. Plenty of people to be found here. As always, the street was crowded with carriages and walkers. Buildings shot up on either side of her in a seemingly endless row ahead. Red, white and brown bricks adorned with signs and colorful paintings, teasing what lay just inside the doors, theatres, studios, shops and offices. Enough sights to draw the attention of even those who'd been born and raised among such. Porri admired them all with amusement. These everyday mundane sights, everyday mundane people, simply fascinated her. Dodging a couple piles of horse manure as she crossed the street, she made her way to her apartment nestled above the bread shop. Wafts of warmth and the smell of yeast soothed her soul while she climbed the stairs. One of the bakers waved when he saw her and hustled over before she could get more than a few steps up.

"Hello! Good evening," he grinned broadly at her.

"Good evening, William. Did you have a busy day, today?" Porri asked. She was tired and ready to get off her feet but didn't want to be rude. William was a nice young man and had always been particularly thoughtful toward her. In fact, she had a notion he may be a little sweet on her. While she certainly didn't entertain the idea or want to encourage it, she disliked the thought of disappointing him.

"I did, in fact!" He seemed very happy about it too. "I baked extra today, may I send you up with a loaf?"

"Oh," Porri's palm pressed to her heart, touched by his generosity, "that really isn't necessary."

"It's no bother," he insisted. Not waiting for her response, he trotted away from her and retrieved a plate from behind the counter then brought it over.

Porri was uncomfortable taking advantage of any affection he might have for her, but she *was* hungry, and the bread smelled so good just now. "Thank you, William. Really. That's very kind of you."

"Anything for the lady," he exaggerated a bow then stood back up with an even wider grin, "there's some fresh butter wrapped up in the cloth as well," he said in a half whisper, partially hiding his mouth with his hand as though someone might overhear.

"Thank you," Porri said again.

"Of course, of course. I won't keep you. Have a lovely evening, Miss." William gave another rather awkward wave as he backed away from her, nearly bumping into a patron.

"You as well, Sir." Porri gave the biggest smile she had in her, then turned and ascended the rest of the stairs. Once inside, Porri set the plate on the little dining table in the center of the room and immediately removed her shoes. She didn't know who came up with the design for these things, but she was pretty sure it wasn't someone who had to wear them. She walked toward the stove, flexing her toes along the way, trying to get the blood flowing back into them. There was still water left in the kettle from this morning, so she lit the fire and walked back across the room to recover her teapot. It was a small apartment, but it suited her fine. The room was full of furnishings. A peach-colored sofa rested against the wall with two tiny footstools in front of it. The side table that had held her teapot sat to its right and just beyond that, the record player. Around the mahogany dining table stood four chairs upholstered in red and gold, and to the left of that, against the other wall, a mahogany piano to match with a red stool. White and gold curtains were draped from the large windows overlooking Princess Street and simple landscape paintings hung on the wall, breaking up the busy green wallpaper and carpeting. The same colors carried through into her bedroom and washroom. Simple. Cozy. And she loved it.

Eyeing the plate on the table, Porri remembered her appetite and began to close in on it when she doubled over. A shockwave of pain shot through her, leaving her stomach and heart throbbing. Reaching out for one of the dining chairs she slowly lowered herself to the seat and closed her eyes. The same emotions that always followed engulfed her. Grief, jealously, resentment and grief again. "Shera," Porri whispered almost inaudibly, a tear falling down her cheek. For a while, she found herself lost in the past, wandering, drifting, to a time nearly beyond memory, when the sudden whistling of the tea kettle brought her crashing back to reality.

CHAPTER 4

The Hanal lui Manuc was stirring as usual. Sal leaned against a wooden beam on the second floor, overlooking the courtyard below. Turkish wholesalers called out to the browsing patrons, holding out their colorful rugs, towels, handmade yarns and leathers while the Romanian booths offered the best dairy, wool, eggs and honey. Within the lower floors of the Inn another 23 shops caried the finest silks from Salonica and West Anatolia as well as the newest fashions for women and jobens for the men, most of whom you could find in clouds of smoke at the pub. If you stared long enough, the buzz of sound and color started to look like a dance.

The square shape of the hotel provided a view of every other room, behind wooden railings and beams supporting beautifully carved archways and staircases. The white paint and roof just made the goods being sold below seem more vibrant and the echoes of laughter more oneiric. He liked this place. Rumor was, it would be serving as the town hall next year as well. Putting the pipe in his mouth, Sal inhaled deeply then looked up at the sky and thought of her. After a moment, he rounded and opened the door behind him, stepping into the room.

Les had brought up a feast from downstairs and Brach was already tearing into it, hungrily. "If I didn't know for certain Reesha was out there, I would swear your better half was food, Brach," Sal chuckled. Brach paused mid-bite and looked up at him, a bit of cabbage clinging to his lower lip.

"I'm hungry," he retorted.

"When are you not hungry?" Les asked, setting down three mugs on the table and gesturing to the empty chair across from him. "Sal?"

Obligingly, Sal sat, taking up a mug and gulping down some of the thick beer. "Thank you, Les."

The table was set with their favorites: ciulama made with lamb and white sauce, sarmale (cabbage leaves stuffed with walnuts and olives) and zacusca, an eggplant chutney, as well as some of the polenta left over from earlier in the day. The food was hot and they ate in silence, each lost in his own thoughts.

Les and Brach had made their way from

Greece to Romania roughly three years ago after the liberalization of commerce on the Danube and the Black Sea made it possible and had arrived here just in time for the flood. Deciding to venture to dryer lands, they moved through Moldova and Austria then circled back through Transylvania before returning to Bucharest. They had found Sal only last month. He was a native but had taken to traveling for nearly a year at a time before returning to prepare for his next trip. Their reunion was definitely not unwelcome to him. Nor, indeed, to any of them. This was always easier when the others were around. Next stop was Russia. Sal had been there before, of course, but it wouldn't hurt to look again for their sake if nothing else.

Les leaned back in his chair, mug in hand, and watched Brach continue to chew. Shaking his head slightly, he wondered at it. He'd lost his taste for food, or rather his enjoyment of it, many years ago. It was nothing more than a necessary means to fuel his body now. Brach, on the other hand..... Les sighed and sipped, letting his mind wander. Allowing himself to remember her scent, her eyes, her energy engulfing him, swelling his heart. Her whispered name on repeat in his head. It had been so long this time. His heart sinking at the familiar thought into dangerous territory, he pushed it aside and cleared his throat. *Focus on the task.* "Did you.." he began.

"It's taken care of," Sal answered without waiting for the question.

Brach let out a sound of incredulousness, carrying a bit of rice to Sal's coat with it. "I thought he said it was full."

"My dear Brach," Sal smiled, flicking the rice off his clothes, "when are you going to learn? My powers of persuasion are next to none."

"Did you persuade us into comfortable quarters?" Brach mirrored Sal's smarmy smile.

Sal, unflinching, replied "in fact I did."

"Cheers to that!" Les held up his mug and tilted it toward Sal.

Grunting, Brach took his own mug and held it up, offering a wink to Sal. The train was a much better option than carriage for the journey. He could sleep. He could dream. He could think of her with less distractions. The food was better too.

"And what about you," Sal asked Brach, "did you secure our accommodations?"

"Yes." Brach pushed his plate away and retrieved a letter from his pocket, handing it to Sal. "I heard back today. Two months of tenancy in Omsk, at least. He also has connections in Irkutsk and Tchuktchi. We're expected the day after tomorrow."

"Very good," Sal nodded.

"Very good," Les repeated. Grabbing two of the plates he stood and then froze, one of the plates falling from his grip and crashing onto the floor. Sal's eyes closed tightly and Brach's arms shot out, gripping the table for support. The silence in the room became deafening. After what seemed an eternity, Les slowly lowered himself back down to his chair and slid the intact plate back onto the table. Sal took a slow, deep breath before meeting Les' eyes then they both looked at Brach, who now had his face in his hands. He stayed that way for a couple of minutes before lowering them to reveal wet eyes.

"Shera," Brach whispered, not so much to Sal and Les as it was a call to her.

Les put his hand over his heart and bowed his head. "We're with you, Cas. We're with you."

CHAPTER 5

Resha stood nervously at the window, gazing up at the sky. Wondering if he was thinking of her. Trying to ignore the tug in her chest. Cannon fire rang out and she crossed her arms.

"It will be fine," Mina reassured her.

"For one of us, perhaps," Resha responded, glancing over at her, "but not for both." She had been glad to find Mina and thought the two of them could be in some sort of peace for a while. As usual, she was mistaken. It seemed they were cursed with bad timing as well. Not four months after she arrived, the war began. The cannon fire from the Pearl River onto Canton could be seen and heard from their Siheyuan in Amoy. The British, her people, were relentless. And wrong. She had seen firsthand the effects opium had been having on the Chinese population. She had seen them wasting away on the streets, shivering and vomiting. The lengths to which they would go in order to get more. According to Mina, that had only gotten worse after the ban. It simply wasn't safe here. Shera sighed, such a beautiful and peaceful country, being ripped apart because of a silver deficit. She had been surprised when Mina's brother allowed her to stay here since everyone else had been banished to Macau and sensed her invitation would not be extended much longer.

Mina's home was at least sheltered amongst the trees, nestled up against the mountain. If there was a place to be forbidden to leave, this was ideal. Mina's brother was in the fight and, aside from the servants, they were alone here. Resha had never seen anything like a Siheyuan. It was spread out in a square shape with six separate wooden buildings and a large courtyard in the middle. The vermillion gate was guarded by a pair of stone lions, and another pair stood by the main entrance beneath giant, copper door knockers. The building to the North was the main house and where Mina's brother slept. They tended to stay away from that area in general. The buildings on either side were bedrooms, but as they were both unmarried women, they had to sleep in one of the buildings to the rear along with the female servants. The courtyard was where Resha preferred to spend her time. Four trees shaded the majority of it, one in each corner and in the center of the crossed pathway stood a lovely stone fountain. The hallways between each building were decorated with statues and provided a place to sit in relative quiet.

The room they were in now, the reception room, was in the Southern building. This is where they ate, talked, read; lived, really. Mina sat at the small tea table in the corner, dwarfed by the massive size of the rectangular room. The large windows provided plenty of sunlight but were shaded with lattice window shutters and beige tapestries depicting women working in the rice fields. A row of camphor wood chairs lined opposite walls, facing each other. They were square and simple aside from the intricate floral designs carved into the base and legs. At the far end of the room a much more ornate set of zitan chairs, inlaid with mother of pearl happiness medallions, sat on either side of a matching table. On taller tables to the right and left were blue and white porcelain vases featuring birds perched on pomegranate trees. And on the wall behind, drawing everyone's attention, a tapestry of Fu Lu Shou and the proclamation "The three stars are present." Resha particularly liked that one. Three men, one in a scholar's dress, holding a scroll, the second in the dress of a mandarin, and the third with a domed forehead, carrying a peach and smiling broadly. Good fortune, prosperity and immortality.

The best thing, however, was the poem beautifully written on the long scrolls which hung on opposite sides of the tapestry. Simply translated it said "the heart is a good field, plow it for a hundred generations and it will never be depleted. Goodness is a perfect treasure, use it for a lifetime and some will remain."

"Resha," Mina called softly. Resha turned, not realizing she'd been lost in her mind again. "Please come sit. Have some tea."

Resha obliged, making her way to the table. Reaching for her teacup she had to flail her arms a bit to get the sleeves out of the way. She found it very hard to function in her aoku. The enormous amount of silk fabric used in this clothing startled her. She was happy to wear it, of course, but it would take some getting used to. She smiled at the memory of the look the servant had given her when Resha refused to let her bind her feet. Evidently her British feet were large and unfeminine, but she wasn't about to torture herself. Mina had laughed so hard it startled the servant who left in a huff.

"Do you do this?" Resha had asked her.

"Unfortunately, I was born to it," Mina replied, still laughing. She was not laughing now, though. In fact, she looked pretty downtrodden.

"I'm….sure your brother will be fine." Resha took her hand.

Mina smiled politely and squeezed it. "That's nice of you to say, but you know that's not what I'm thinking about."

"I know." Resha released her hand and slouched in her chair. "I don't believe the chance of us getting onto a ship has improved any."

Another round of cannon fire echoed in the distance and Mina winced. "If this keeps up, we may not live to find them anyway."

"Don't think like that," Resha urged. "They may yet find *us*."

Mina stood, restlessly looking about the room. Her eyes fell upon the jade incense burner pot and she moved to refill it. Resha reeled.

Between the endless incense and the scent of the camphor wood, her sense of smell was on overload. She needed some fresh air. "Let's go into the courtyard."

Mina shrugged and put the incense down. "Alright," she said. The sound of the fountain always calmed her. Her heart ached in desperation and helplessness. The isolation of this place only made it worse. Resha hadn't been here long enough to really understand that. She had, at least, gotten to travel. Mina was not even permitted in public. Her brother was a good man, but the traditions of this culture were harsh to her. She knew she'd have to leave before she was forced to marry. Resha finding her was the beacon of light she'd been hoping for. She finally had a way out. Then, the war. She wondered how many more years would go by without him this time.

Turning, she saw Resha was by the door, hand extended out to her. Mina took a deep breath. At the very least, she wasn't alone anymore. As she took Resha's hand and they started through the door, both were hit with a tidal wave of gut-wrenching pain. Resha doubled over and let out a cry while Mina's arms covered her head. "No.... no, no, no." Hot tears flooded her eyes and Resha hugged her tightly. They stood in each other's arms, rocked by grief, weeping for her.... for them.

CHAPTER 6

The blistering sun beat down on Nunki through the open window, and a bead of sweat dripped down her brow. She wanted to venture further out, to feel the breeze, to join the crowd gathered on the pier, watch the fisherman bringing in their catch and dip her feet into the sea. Unfortunately, there wasn't time. They'd be back soon.

It was quiet the view from their little apartment there at the end of Heerengracht Street. Their building was just tall enough to see over the massive white roof and steeple of the Groote Kerke and onto the bustling street beyond. Heerengracht was Cape Town's main road and busiest area. Most of the businesses, apartments, shops and entertainment venues were spread from where she was to the ocean. A yell caught her attention and she noticed a gentleman balancing two buckets of what looked to be fish on either end of a long staff over his shoulders, like a milk maid. He was cursing and doing his best to shake his fist at the careless driver of a passing carriage without dropping his goods. As the carriage moved away from him, Nunki could just make out the Holt & Holt sign hanging from its back. A heavy-set woman in a blue skirt and white blouse waved down at the driver from her third floor balcony whilst fanning herself.

Once again, Nunki found herself wishing she'd found a place with a balcony. Not that there was anything really wrong with this place. It was comfortable. Big enough. Light. Simple. The living space she sat in housed a large, rectangular wooden table and four chairs under an iron chandelier, a brick inglenook fireplace with a cast iron stove, woodpile, and various cooking pots, a wash basin by the kitchen window, and a sitting area by the other window where Nunki was. The walls were made of white panels that were contrasted by the dark wooden beams and furniture. There was also a washroom and two bedrooms. She'd been told, when searching for the apartment five months prior, that all the nicer places were occupied. Nearly everywhere she went, she'd been turned away or told to check down at the end of the street. She expected her dark skin had something to do with it. Slavery had been abolished a whole six years prior and, even though there were as many blacks as whites here, a sort of racial tension she didn't understand remained. And the majority of the businesses on the street were still under British or Dutch control. The Town Municipality had been formed just before she arrived in Cape Town and seemed to be taking steps to address the racial issues, but progress was slow. And if Nunki had learned anything over the years it was that you can't quell the ignorant hatred out of man. Or love, for that matter. She took a deep breath and looked up at the sky, whispering his name quietly in her head.

The door opened suddenly, and Maia entered, followed by Dorsum. "Success!" Maia exclaimed as Dorsum set a large bundle wrapped in cheesecloth on the table.

"On more than one count, I hope." Nunki's palms pressed together in a prayer position as she waited for the response.

"Yes," Maia returned with a smile.

Dorsum nodded, removing his hat and rolling up his sleeves. "My man at the lighthouse managed to get us all passage next week."

Nunki let out a sigh of relief. She tried to take another deep breath but found the cheesecloth-covered parcel too pungent and rose to help prepare dinner. She set to peeling potatoes while Maia ground the spices and chopped onion and Dorsum began deboning and cleaning the fish in a tub. They worked in relative silence. Each thinking of their own hopes for the coming months.

Maia had almost gone with the rest of her people during their mass migration North a couple of years ago. But, from the moment she'd arrived in Cape Town with her family, she'd felt Nunki's presence somewhere not too far away. She'd elected to stay behind , working in one of the Dutch pastry shops and had taken to wandering the streets in her spare time in hopes of finding her. Finally, during one of her wanderings, Maia came around a corner and there she was. The elation at finding her friend was indescribable. Nunki, a native of South Africa, had lost much of her family to the slave trade and slowly made the move to Cape Town with a group of people looking for a safer life. They had both been and felt very much alone when they found one another, and decided to take up residence off the main road while they formulated a plan. Maia had been staying in a shared living space with other woman and had only a bed. So their best bet was to get an apartment, which Nunki looked for while Maia continued to work. Low and behold, within a few months of their securing an apartment, Dorsum arrived on a vessel from Australia. He'd known they were close as soon as the ship drew near to the coast, just as they'd felt *him* approaching. Their reunion, as always, was sweet.

Maia glanced at Dorsum, his tanned skin and thick hair the color of sand, then looked down at her own pale body and smiled. Her thoughts turned briefly to Mina then, as always, to him. Her Les. Choking down the temptation to think the worst if this time around, she doubled her efforts with the onion chopping and tried to push him from her mind.

Noticing the sudden aggression with which Maia was knifing that poor vegetable, Dorsum started for a moment. Taking in her platinum hair, pale skin and thin frame. It didn't suit her. She looked fragile. This woman was anything but fragile. Nunki, on the other hand, was beautiful, dark, and exuded strength. He was so grateful that he'd found them. He knew he needed to be there with them and for them. The world these days was not especially kind towards women. Even these women, as extraordinary as they were, would face more challenges than he. They would stick together. Together they would find.... He paused and closed his eyes, letting himself feel her energy... sometimes, if he just allowed himself to open up, he could feel her there with him. Then he clenched his jaw and, following Maia's lead, set into gutting the fish with new fervor.

Without warning pain shot to his head and the knife slipped from his hand. Nunki gasped loudly and Maia stumbled backward until she hit the window then lowered herself down to the window sill. Dorsum fell into the chair next to him and Nunki leaned on the table. Not a word was spoken nor sound could be heard other than Maia's soft sobbing. After a minute Nunki's eyes met Dorsum's, agony in each. Why did this never get easier?

CHAPTER 7: PRESENT DAY

Quiet. Black. Nothing. Shera floated there, in the vastness of space. Oddly comforted by her surroundings, the glittering of distant stars and that giant, blue sphere before her. Fragile and awe-inspiring. Earth had always been especially lovely to her from this view. Calling to her in its silence, the light almost reaching out to embrace her. She'd had this dream how many times over the years? It never failed to bring her a sense of peace, a sense of... home. She could hear nothing but her breath. Slow, steady, calm. This was where she belonged.

Suddenly a chill ran through her body. Not because of the cold, she couldn't feel the cold. She was dreaming. This was....wait... there was something different this time. Her stomach tensed and the hair on her neck stood up. Something was... she looked around and saw nothing out of the ordinary. *What the hell is that?* she thought. Starting to panic, she looked around more frantically. The surrounding silence gave way to the thud of her heart, and her breath grew faster, more shallow. She wasn't alone out here. Not this time. Someone was with her. Starting to flail her limbs, she tried in vain to turn around. Whoever it was, she could sense them behind her. Something that felt like a long nail touched the back of her neck at the base of her skull and slowly dragged downward to her shoulders. She tried to yell out, but the sound wasn't right. It was as though she was screaming under water. Her ears were plugged and everything was distant. She yelled again, the same muffled noise came out. All at once a deep, loud, guttural growl surrounded her. It was clear as a bell, terrifyingly slow and entirely unnatural.

"Shit. Shit!" she said aloud, helpless. There was no way out of here. She blinked her eyes repeatedly. *Wake up!* she thought. *Wake the fuck up!* The growling intensified and the darkness around her grew darker still. Her heart was going to pound out of her chest. "What the hell is it? What do you want?" she yelled. "Shit!"

Out of nowhere the growl morphed into a blood curdling scream, like a thousand people being burned alive. It was so loud her brain rattled in her skull and her hands impulsively went to her ears. Unable to turn her head, Shera could see something forming in her peripheral, a mist so dark and thick it almost seemed solid. It swirled around, making its way more and more into her sightline. She could see the beginnings of a face and a burning red eye. Her blood froze. It was close enough to kiss her. She could feel its rancid breath on her cheek. *Wake up, wake up, wake up*, she begged herself. She held her breath, just then, it lunged.

Shera's eyes shot open and her body jerked upward. Looking around, panicked, she saw that she was in her room. She exhaled and collapsed back onto her pillow. "What the fuck?" she said aloud. Throwing back her blanket, her hand ran over the sheets. They were soaked through with sweat. She rubbed her face trying to erase the image from her mind, her heart still beating abnormally fast. "What the fuck was that?" she asked herself again, exasperated. "Not cool!" She lay there, staring at the ceiling fan whirling above her head. She had had that dream a million times. Never, never had something like this happened. The growl still echoed in her ears. And that face, sweet mother of Zeus, that face...she shivered. Taking deep breaths, she tried to slow her heart. A strange feeling began to nag at her. *This isn't right,* she thought. *Something isn't right.* Letting the nightmare replay over and over in her head, the nagging grew stronger. At last, she sat up. Her cell phone suddenly buzzed. She picked it up knowing exactly who the text was going to be from.

We need to meet. London. Planetarium. S.

Shera half smiled down at the message. "Ok. Not a nightmare, then." She tossed the phone on the bed and stood up. "London. Naturally. Always gets the good spots."

She wondered what he was doing now. Padding into the kitchen she squinted slightly at the sunlight coming through then set about making coffee. Better make it a bit stronger today, adding an extra scoop to the filter and flicking it on. Taking a deep breath, she listened to the sound of the percolator perking to life. It was like music to her ears. Alright, she had a minute. Trying to ignore the jitters that had now taken over her body, she sat down at her laptop. "Now, lets buy a plane ticket to London, shall we?" she said aloud in her best, and truly terrible British accent.

CHAPTER 8

The words on the pages in front of her blurred. *I should probably turn the page*, Shera thought. She flipped the page then tried to look as though she was intently reading instead of absent mindedly staring at the book in front of her face. What the hell was she even reading, anyway? Glancing up at the title. *A Brief History of Thought*. Ah, now she remembered. She had grabbed it at a used bookstore last week, seemed a bit superfluous, but it had interested her at the time. There is no history of thought, she scowled, people are born, they exist, they try to understand that existence, they fail to do so and then they die. *There. I summed it up. I can't imagine why they didn't ask me to contribute to the dust cover.* She took a deep breath. She wanted to look again. She shouldn't. She shouldn't even be here, really. Grabbing the coffee that had been sitting on the bench and leaning against her leg, she took a drink and let her eyes wander up.

The playground was full of children, their laughs, screams and taunts echoed around her along with the faint murmur of the mothers who had gathered to gossip. Careful not to turn her head, Shera searched the corner of her vision for his face. He stood behind the swing set, pushing a squealing child just a bit higher than was probably safe.

"Not so high!" a young woman yelled at them from another bench.

"He's fine," the man smiled back. "Look at him, he loves it."

Shera fought the urge to grin, knowing full well the look she would see on the woman's face if she allowed herself. Imagining herself being able to share in the reaction. *What did you expect?* she would have said to her. A hint of familiar longing began to brew in her stomach. What she wouldn't give, if only for a single conversation. She shook her head, allowing her gaze to return to the man and immediately stopped breathing. *Shit.* He was staring back. *Shit.* She looked away quickly. She was being careless. It was time for her to leave. She slammed the book shut, shoved it into the backpack at her feet and stood. He was still watching her, she could feel it. Throwing the pack over her shoulder and clenching her coffee, she hurriedly walked away. Feeling his gaze burning into her back as the squeals of delight faded into traffic noise behind her.

CHAPTER 9

The Planetarium was not really what she's expected. Approaching it from the outside, it looked more like some sort of missile silo. A leaning, steel cylinder sitting atop a modest concrete structure. Seemingly out of place with the surrounding brick buildings. Making her way down the stairs and toward the lobby, she saw a bus screech to a halt and open its doors. Resembling a wounded insect, bleeding tourists equipped with cameras and pre-conceived wonder. *They must be here for the next show.* Shera sped her pace and pushed through the doors before the tourists could start flooding in. A woman stood behind the lobby desk. Shera smiled charmingly.

"Hello," she said.

"Good afternoon," the woman offered back. "Are you here for the show?"

"No," Shera replied, "actually, I'm here to meet a friend of mine, Sadal Arun?"

"Yes, of course," the woman said, lighting up a bit. "He's just brilliant. He should be wrapping up about now."

"Wrapping up?" Shera questioned.

"Yes," the woman said again. "Wrapping up with his class. He comes in to give a lecture for the university once a week."

Shera smiled, *so he's teaching people about the stars, of course he was.* "Would you mind if I just wait for him to finish inside?" Shera asked, pointing to the doors leading into the auditorium. "I've never seen him lecture before."

"We're really not supposed to let people in," she replied in a whisper then leaned in. "But I'll let you go. It would be a shame to miss. He's just wonderful."

Shera laughed to herself. *Sly dog.* "Thank you so much," she said to the woman. "I'll be quiet as a mouse."

She walked to the doors and squeezed the handle as quietly as possible. Pushing ever so slightly, she opened the door barely a crack, not wanting to let any light in. Slipping in through the tiny entrance, she let the door shut softly behind her and was suddenly emerged in darkness. Or what would be darkness, if not for the vast array of stars around her. The cold of the room hit her and for a split second she was transported back to her dream, drifting in space. The hair on the back of her neck stood up and she half expected to hear a growl. Instead, she heard a familiar tone. Relief flooded her and she leaned back against the doors.

"The ecliptic path of the Sun passes through these constellations every year. Yes, they *are* actual constellations and not just the means to an end. I'm not looking at you, but I'm looking at you, Travis." Sadal joked as the class giggled. "Gemini, Pisces, Taurus, Aries, Cancer and Leo. The Eastern celestial hemisphere. Aquarius, Libra, Scorpius, Virgo, Capricornus and Sagittarius, the Western celestial hemisphere."

The countless stars around them narrowed and focused in on the two hemispheres. Lines appeared connecting one to the other. Shera took in the beauty, choking back the lump rising in her throat.

"Opposite sides of the same coin," Sadal continued. "From this view, they almost look close enough to touch each other. Don't they? But, in reality...." He drifted off for a moment. "An ocean of stars, forever in sight..." His gaze fell to where Shera stood against the doors. She knew he felt her there, even in the darkness. "And forever out of reach," he ended. "Class dismissed."

The lights slowly flickered on. Some of the students groaned, rubbing their eyes. Others discretely woke fellow students who had been sleeping. The room stood and Shera moved to the side as the kids started trickling out. She finally brushed past the last few and walked toward Sadal. His back was to her while he packed his briefcase.

"Astrology, really?" she smirked.

Without turning, he laughed. "Seemed appropriate." Closing his briefcase, he rested it on a chair and turned to look at her. They looked at one another for a minute then earnestly embraced. "The years have been good to you, my friend," she said, still hugging him tightly.

"Haven't they?" he joked. He released her and grabbed her by the shoulders to look at her again. "It is good to see you, Shera. You need food."

Taken aback for a second, she suddenly remembered it had actually been a while since she'd eaten and she was undoubtedly pale. She nodded in agreement. "Food."

He reached back and grabbed the strap of his suitcase, pulled it over his shoulder then offered her his arm. Together they walked out of the empty auditorium and into the swell of tourists.

CHAPTER 10

Sadal's apartment didn't seem so much like an apartment as it did a library. In fact, were it not for the kitchen and bedroom, one would probably assume that's where they were. All the walls were lined with bookshelves, stacked floor-to-ceiling with a rolling ladder attached. In the center of the living area sat a large, wooden table complete with an extra lamp, magnifying glass and iron bookstand. There were benches around the table and two worn, brown armchairs on the far side of the room, between which stood a small table and another lamp. No sign of a television. The blinds were all raised, letting in what was left of the day light. The golden rays catching tiny specs of floating dust. Shera was amazed at how similar his places had always looked. Somehow, he'd always managed.

"Would it kill you to have a TV?" Shera kidded. She turned on her barstool to face Sadal who stood chopping vegetables in front of her.

"I prefer to utilize my time in a more appropriate fashion," he retorted. The tea kettle behind him began to whistle. Moving a pile of mushrooms to one side of the cutting board and resting the knife, he turned to pour the hot water into two cups. He set her cup in front of her, tea tag dangling over the side. "Also, it's in the bedroom."

She laughed and took a sip of her tea, feeling him judging her because she hadn't let it steep long enough. Personally, she preferred something a little stronger than tea at the moment, but she knew Sadal had a thing for the stuff and let it go. *Wow, this shit is terrible*, she gagged a bit setting her cup down and letting her hands rest on it. *At least it's warm.* Her fingers tapped the ceramic while Sadal started in on the carrots.

"I know you don't need to ask me why I told you to come," he said without looking at her. She didn't answer, but her heartbeat sped and she clenched her jaw. There was silence for a minute before he continued. "If you haven't seen it, you've felt it." Still she said nothing. He stopped chopping and looked at her. "Did you feel it?"

Shera took a breath, not wanting to dive into this yet. As though by not acknowledging it she could make it disappear. "The disturbance in the force?" she tried to joke.

"No, the twitch in my ass," he returned, sarcastically. Dumping the vegetables into the pan on the stove. Then looking back at her seriously, "Sher, I've never felt anything like this before."

"I'm sorry, are we talking about the twitch?" she said, knowing it amused neither of them, then nodded. "I know. I know. Neither have I. I'm not sure if... maybe I saw it."

"You did? How? What is it?" he prodded.

"I can't even begin to answer that. It was a dream. And I didn't really *see* anything, at least not fully." She said. "But I heard it." The look on her face must have been enough to frighten him because he stared at her then reached out and took her hand. She closed her eyes and squeezed his hand back, feeling a rush of emotion. She spent her life alone, doing everything alone, facing everything alone. Ordinarily, she didn't mind it, even managed it quite well. But this was different. The second she had that dream she felt she was standing on the edge of a cliff and something was trying to pull her off. As if reading her thoughts, Sadal placed his other hand on top of their clasp.

"You're not alone," he assured her, "I'm with you. We all are."

Shera released the breath she hadn't realized she'd been holding in and nodded. "It's really good to see you, Sadal."

Dropping it for the moment, Sadal returned his attention to making dinner. The conversation turned to books and politics as they ate. Both of them seemed perfectly willing to avoid the topic that had actually brought them here, until unavoidable. Once they had eaten and the silence crept back in, Shera relented.

"Has anyone..." She began.

"You're the first," Sadal stated, cutting her off. It would have been impossible for Shera not to notice his expression. She knew it all too well. That sadness, tinged with hope, tinged with dread. Her stomach dropped, leaving her momentarily nauseous as she remembered the difficult admission that was inevitably ahead. A knock at the door startled both of them. "Evidently not by much." Sadal continued as he got up. Swinging the giant green door open a tall, handsome, young man stepped through.

"Sadal," he said cordially. He did a quick survey of the room then walked to the stove and picked a piece of mushroom out of the pan with his fingers, followed by another.

"Come on in," Sadal said, shutting the door. "Help yourself."

"Well, I'm hungry," the man replied in a thick Scottish accent. Shera laughed to herself. *Scottish, how perfect.* Brach had never been one for formalities. He noticed her chuckle. "Shera. Should've known you'd beat me."

"Brachium. It's nice to see you too," she smiled. She really had missed him.

"You look well, Lass." He smiled back at her.

"Thanks, B." She grabbed her plate took it to Sadal who tried to hand a clean one to Brach. Shaking his head, Brach just gestured for a fork. Relenting, Sadal opened the utensil drawer.

"You're a neanderthal," he stated, handing Brach a fork which he then used to eat the remaining food out of the pan.

"I know," Brach returned through a full mouth.

Shera watched with amusement as the pair danced around the kitchen, Sadal trying to clean and Brach constantly side-stepping out of his way while eating from the pan. Finally, Sadal took the empty pan from Brach and started to clean it.

"Nobody else yet?" Brach asked, making his way over to the table to join Shera.

"We haven't heard from her," Shera said to him, understanding what he had really been asking.

He nodded and looked at Sadal. "Porri?"

"Not yet," Sadal said, seeming nervous.

Brach turned back to Shera. "I guess no Cass yet either."

Shera didn't say anything, her jaw clenched again as she stared at the floor. *Dammit*, she thought. She really didn't want to talk about this.

"Shera?" Sadal hadn't brought Cass up because it had always been a hard topic, but this wasn't her usual reaction. "Shera?" he pushed when she didn't answer again.

Shera's stomach turned. *Just say it.* "Cas won't be coming."

Brach looked confused. "Why the hell not? How do you know?"

Shera shrugged and closed her eyes. "The last time..." she hesitated. *How do I tell them?*

Sadal, worried, pressed her. "Shera, what..."

"He chose the vow," she blurted before he could finish. The room went dead quiet. So quiet. Like everyone in it had stopped breathing. Stopped moving. Stopped existing. She opened her eyes half expecting to find she was alone. Sadal had gone almost pale and Brach just stared at her, bewildered. She expected neither of them knew exactly what to say. Her neck felt hot and her palms clammy. A sea of agony threatening to jump out of her. She closed her fists on her lap as her gaze fell to the floor again.

"Are you joking?" Sadal broke the silence. "Seriously, Sher, are you having a laugh?"

"No," she said matter-of-factly. Sadal walked to her and knelt in front of her then put his finger under her chin, raising her eyes to meet his. She understood, he needed to see that she was telling the truth. "No," she said again. In his face she could see a reflection of her own pain mixed with utter disbelief. Then came the rage.

"Bastard," he seethed through gritted teeth.

"Total bastard," Brach added, regaining the use of his speech.

"Stop," Shera pleaded. "He didn't... he wasn't trying to..." she couldn't find the words. *They should understand.* They both knew exactly what it was like and hearing their hatred for him cut into her. "He couldn't do it anymore. "

"None of us want to do it!" Sadal yelled. "But choosing the vow..." He got up and started pacing.

"Seriously, Shera." Brach agreed. "He's a fucking coward. How could he do that to you?"

She had never seen either of them this angry before. It might have been touching if it were under different circumstances. These two had always been particularly protective of her, especially Sadal. But she couldn't handle this. She didn't want them to hate him. "Please," she begged "please. I can't blame him."

"And yet you didn't *join* him," Sadal said forcing himself to calm.

No, she didn't. She could never. Life would

lose it's meaning to her. "A memory is better than nothing," she said, almost to herself. The room was quiet again. "I need a drink."

"That you do," Brach agreed. He picked up her tea cup and smelled it. "What the hell is this?" he tilted the cup to Sadal.

"Tumeric tea," Sadal replied.

"Oh fuck that," Brach shook his head and stood.

Sadal nodded, "There's a bar down the street." He held his hand out signaling Shera to come. Relieved, she stood and followed Brach out, Sadal trailing behind to lock the door.

CHAPTER 11

The whiskey burned its way down her throat, hit her stomach, then covered her body like a warm blanket. *Thank the stars for Brach*, she thought, closing her eyes and disappearing for a moment. A horn rang out from traffic, jolting her back as the cars on her right started to move. It was a cool night, allowing the trio a bit of privacy on the bar patio, the busy street serving to mask any conversation from unwanted ears. They maintained light exchanges, as though they all wanted to keep the dread in their stomachs at bay. Trivial as their lives seemed, there were stories to tell. Good, sad, funny, ... tragic. Shera imagined the series of books they might write. They couldn't, of course, but if they could.......

Staring at her friends she mused, these were the best ones yet. Sadal's face was kind and handsome. His skin smooth and the color of milk chocolate, his eyes two different shades of blue. He was small, but well built, well-groomed with broad shoulders and an air of confidence. Brach, a stark contrast, was tall and pale. Still handsome, but in a less comforting and more assertive way. His strong jaw was offset by piercing green eyes and his hair was as disheveled as his clothing. As she looked at him, Shera noticed his body go rigid and the hand holding his glass begin to shake slightly. He set his glass on the table, brow furrowed. Knowing exactly what was happening, Shera's gaze darted in every direction until it fell on a woman across the street. The woman stood motionless, her concentration fixed on Brach's back, her expression a copy of his. Her ebony skin darker than the night and long, brown hair billowing in the breeze. After what seemed like forever, Brach stood and turned. The atmosphere around them seemed to change, become electric, as though bolts of lightning were shooting back and forth between the pair of them. He walked to the edge of the sidewalk while, without looking, she made her way across and stood before him. Her chest heaving and visibly shaken, her brown eyes welled with tears. Neither one of them seemed to be able to move. Time stood still. At last, they intensely embraced. Shera's hand automatically reached out for Sadal's. Fear, joy, envy and sadness gripped them both as they remained riveted on the couple. They waited, watching the embrace, Shera's heart pounding.

"Please," she begged. "Please don't."

Hearing her, Sadal gripped her hand more tightly. "Shera...." He trailed off. His attention now on everything surrounding them. "I don't think.... something is different....."

Taking a deep breath and letting it out slowly, Shera barely dared to hope. She expected a car to come out of nowhere and barrel toward the two, a mugger, the ground to open beneath them. But nothing..... nothing was happening. After a moment, a light started to emit from the couple, faint, but noticeable. Nervous, Shera turned her focus to the people around them, some of whom were beginning to stare.

"We should go," Sadal suggested. Shera nodded in agreement and they stood. Sadal threw some cash on the table and they quickly strode toward Brach and the woman. Seeing them, she beamed.

"Resha," Shera almost whispered, emotional. Putting her arm around her friend and bringing their foreheads carefully together.

Sadal took Resha's hand, while around Shera's back and grasped Brach's shoulder. "It's good to see you," he said to Resha who was still crying, seeming beyond the words that were unnecessary. Turning to Brach, he quietly instructed his attention to the audience they were drawing. Brach simply nodded, pulled Resha close to his side and, together, they all made their way back to Sadal's in silence.

As the elevator rose to Sadal's floor, a feeling began to grip all four of them. A familiar, distant feeling almost forgotten. It strengthened with each inch upward. Shera didn't know for certain what she would see when they stepped out of the elevator, but she could very easily guess. And it should be impossible. As the elevator came to a halt, all of them stopped breathing. The seconds between the stop, the clear ding of the signaling elevator, and the opening of the doors seemed much longer than they should have, especially to them. As soon as the doors began to crack open, a strange, faint beam of light filled the growing space. As daylight penetrates the clouds during a rainstorm. Passing the threshold into the illuminated hall, the sight that greeted them was one they had never seen. Six people, standing in pairs, each holding onto the other as though existence itself relied upon one-another's grasp. A beautiful, glowing light reflecting off each pair, creating a prism effect in the hallway. Like sunlight through a crystal. Shera could feel her heart both bursting and breaking. Her family was together again. Almost.

For a long time, all anyone could do was stand there. Looking at each other. Communicating through unspoken words. The silence was broken only when the elevator behind them let out a familiar ding. Shera's heart leapt. *Porri.* She could nearly feel Sadal's pulse quicken beside her. They turned to see a beautiful, almost fragile looking woman come through the doors. Wearing a light blue dress that showed her slender and delicate frame, her black hair tied up in a bun. Porri's eyes immediately found Sadal's. He forced himself to take a deep breath then rushed toward her and took her in his arms. Shera smiled. Of all the things she could wish for her dearest friend, this was what she wanted for him most. The light in the hallway grew brighter, bathing everyone in a rainbow of color.

CHAPTER 12

Nikki leaned back in his chair and raised the coffee to his lips. Surveying the monitors before him until satisfied that there was nothing out of the ordinary, he took out his phone and scrolled through his emails. Nothing new. Letting out an audible sigh, he clicked it off and returned it to his pocket. He'd spent a year trying to get this job at Nasa. And while he couldn't complain about the salary, he had to admit he'd romanticized the role a bit. Monitoring satellite images probably wasn't going to earn him the title of space hero or famous explorer, but he had hoped, at least, for a discovery of some kind. Was it so much to ask that he be the one person to point out an anomaly that had been entirely overlooked by everyone of consequence and end up saving the world as we know it?

Thanks to the keen eyes and quick action of Nikolas Calcareon, he thought to himself, *the world has been spared. Nikolas, for all those watching, would you tell us what you felt in those first moments?* "Well, Karen," he said aloud, "I'd like to say that

I'm no hero. Just an ordinary man, doing my job. And in the first moments..."

A quiet alarm grabbed his attention. Lights next to the monitor on his right began to blink in time with the beeping. Using his keyboard to gain access to the satellite's camera, he started panning it around. What was going on? He didn't see anything wrong. He tried moving the camera in another direction, then immediately froze. *What the hell?* There was a formation, not more than 10 feet from the camera, of what looked like a black mist. He leaned in closer to the monitor and tried to zoom in. He hadn't ever seen anything like this. He wouldn't believe his eyes, but for the veiling of stars in that area. It was just floating there. Still, but in constant motion. It looked almost like it was in the shape of ...... but it couldn't be. He leaned in more, drawn in by it. Then, without warning, it rushed the camera. Nikki jolted backward, his chair rolling. The monitor now showed nothing but static. Shaking his head in disbelief, Nikki tried to think for a second. *What do I do?*

"Fuck," he said, reaching for the phone. Whatever this was, it was above his pay grade.

CHAPTER 13

This is unreal, Shera thought. Every inch of Sadal's living room was dancing with color as the couples sat spread over the room. Brach and Resha shared a lounge chair while Nunki sat in the other, Sal on the floor in front of her and leaning back between her legs, her fingers running through his ginger hair. Nunki was a stunning Puerto Rican. Thin with smooth skin and a bobbed cut on her glossy, brown hair. Sal was pale and thin, with thick glasses. A self-proclaimed genius from ... where was it... New Zealand?

Les and Maia sat around the table in the center of the room with Dorsum and Mina. Les, with dark skin and a bald head, hailed from Lebanon. And Maia, tall and strongly built with caramel-colored curls, called Ukraine home. Dorsum was an older, well dressed German, and Mina a small, sweet, elderly Chinese woman with long, peppered hair.

Shera sat on a stool at the kitchen counter, admiring them all. These bodies all suited somehow. Sadal and Porri stood, locked in each other's arms in the kitchen. There was a peace pervading the room that none of them had experienced in a very, very long time.

"We should probably get started," Sadal announced.

Nunki chimed in, "Aren't we missing one? Shouldn't we wait for Cas?"

Sadal's jaw tightened, but Shera just shook her head. "No, we can go ahead."

"But Shera..." Maia started.

"Sadal?" Shera interrupted her. Sadal exchanged looks with Brach then proceeded. "Ok, we should probably start with what everyone knows so far."

The room was silent for a moment. It seemed nobody really knew how to explain their experiences. Resha was the first to speak up. "I'm not sure I *know* anything. I can tell you it's dark. Like, negative. But it's just a feeling, you know? I can't... I can just say how I feel ... and it came out of nowhere."

Les nodded. "Same. My first thought was Zeus."

"It's not Zeus." Sal stated matter of factly. The room went silent again while everyone looked at Sal. He sat relishing the focus. Sal was never one to shy away from flaunting his intellect. He held the pause as long as he could then added, "Not only is this not him, but it's stronger."

Porri leaned on the counter. "How do you know?"

"Two things," Sal continued, "first, the frequency. It tapped into all of us at least a day ago and I think we can all agree it is not coming from anywhere on the planet. Then there's the obvious second..."

"We're all still here," Mina said.

Sal scowled at the theft of his thunder, but nodded. "Yes. Forgetting our halves for a minute, when was the last time we were all together? In the same place at the same time? Not only are we still alive but we were *intentionally* brought together because..."

"He needs us for something," Mina jumped in again.

"You want to stop doing that?" Sal blurted.

"Sorry," Mina replied, casting a glance to Shera. Shera, spotting the ever so slight grin on Mina's face had to lower her head to hide her own.

"Are you seriously suggesting Zeus is afraid of something?" Maia asked.

"You mean besides Hera," Brach jokingly added, earning a look from Maia that prompted him to put his hands up in surrender.

Resha reached out and lowered his hand in front of her face. "So what do we do?" she asked the room. Again, silence.

Shera took a deep breath. "Nothing," she said. "We don't know enough to do anything right now. We sit tight. Dorsum?" He looked at her. "You mentioned you were courting the heads of the Aerospace Center."

"Courting? No, no. I own their balls. Their balls are right here." He held up his hand and indicated his palm.

Shera smiled, "Well, thank you for that visual. Do you think you could maybe fondle less and squeeze more tomorrow? It sounds strange, but... I believe we need eyes out there." She nodded toward the window.

Brach tilted his head, "Do you think we're actually going to see something out there?"

"Shera?" Maia prodded, "what aren't you saying?"

"Nothing. I may have seen..... something.... It's probably nothing. It was just a dream and I don't want to jump to conclusions yet." Shera tried to ignore the stares. "It's precaution, that's all."

Nunki's voice relieved Shera of the attention. "Has anyone else had... sorry... ," she was gripping her head as though in a vice, "... there's this buzzing. It's been getting louder."

"I hear it too," Mina said. "But it's not a buzzing. It's more like..."

"Growling," Shera, Resha and Sadal all said together. Silence crept over them again. Shera's mind shot back to her dream, the terrifying growl pervading her brain and giving her goosebumps. Nobody knew what else to say. Finally Sadal chimed in.

"Ok, everyone take the night. I know I don't need to say it but stay with your halves. We'll meet back here tomorrow."

There was a sudden feeling of excitement in the room. Almost disbelief. None of them had had so much as seconds with their halves for longer than most humans could fathom. In each of these broken souls lingered centuries of grief and longing. The idea of being whole again was nearly too much. Shera looked around the room as everyone started standing, then got up to leave, catching Mina's eye.

"Shera," she called, walking quickly to her friend and taking her hand. "Brach told me."

Shera gripped Mina's hand tightly. "It's ok, Mina, I'm ok."

"Have you seen him?"

"Yeah, actually. Turns out I can spend as much time around him as I want as long as he doesn't recognize me," Shera blurted, bitter at the irony. "He's happy. I saw him yesterday, playing with his grandson."

Mina tensed, "He... he had a ... what? ... He has a child?"

"A daughter," Shera said, a mix of sadness and pride dancing behind her eyes. "I guess the vow is not without it's benefits."

Mina's eyes welled with tears and she threw her arms around Shera, hugging her as tightly as possible. Shera tried choking back her own emotions. She didn't want to break down here. "He's happy, Mina," she half whispered to her friend, as though it was all the justification she needed. "He's happy."

CHAPTER 14

They're shrouded tonight, he thought, instinctively squinting as though it would enable him to see the stars better through his reflection in the window. He always felt uneasy when he couldn't see them clearly. His focus wandered to the figure staring back at him. He saw a man there in the glass, 5'10", firmly built, self assured, hands tucked in his jean pockets as though he hadn't a care in the world. Cas was familiar enough with that face. The strong jaw, slightly pointed nose and neatly kept beard, all emphasizing that sad, sometimes lost expression. Yet, for some reason, every time he saw that face gazing out of the mirror, he felt he was looking at someone else entirely. He tried to calm himself. He'd been on some sort of adrenaline roller coaster for the last couple days and the anxiety was starting to wear on him. Not to mention having absolutely no idea why he was so on edge only made it worse. There was a sort of tug on his core. Like he was being pulled. As to where or why...?

He took a deep breath and let it out slowly

as he looked back up. He could almost hear them, the stars, inaudible whispers in his head. Over the years he'd grown so accustomed to the sound that he barely noticed it anymore. Except now. There was something different. Almost like static, white noise on top of the whispers. His head cocked slightly to the right while he leaned in closer to the window. What was that? The hair on the back of his neck stood up as it grew steadily louder. *It sounds like... something... is gr...*

"Dad?" Cas was startled out of his thoughts. Lilian stood behind him, putting her coat on. She had paused midway through and appeared slightly concerned.

"Yeah," he replied.

"You ok?" she asked.

"Of course."

Lilian was a pretty, young woman. Tall like Cas, but she had inherited her mother's blonde hair and blue eyes. And, just like her mother, he felt them frequently judging him. "You didn't hear me calling you?" She put on the remainder of her coat and inched closer.

"No, sorry. I've got this... buzzing in my ear."

Cas palmed his left ear a couple of times as if trying to knock the sound loose.

"You sure you're ok?" Lilian asked again. "We can stick around for a bit, make you dinner."

"No, no. I'm good, Sweety," he assured her with a smile. *Unlike* her mother, she was an incredibly caring woman. "I'll see you this weekend."

Lilian raised an eyebrow, clearly not convinced, but she knew better than to argue with him. She reached down and grabbed a child's coat off the armchair. The room was dark, illuminated only by a small lamp on the side table. Cas had always been a bit of a minimalist. A simply gray sofa and chair sat in front of the window and a modern, glass coffee table displayed a mint condition book on Antiques of the Ancient World. The only other furniture in the room was a shiny, black grand piano, sitting stoically in the corner. It was a spacious formal living room that had never really been used for family living. While the fancy, built in bar allowed it to be the center of a few gatherings, it was largely untouched by anyone except himself. Oddly, despite being the darkest and chilliest room in the house, it was Cas's favorite. It was his thinking room. His truth room. The one place he could go where there was nothing to distract him from facing himself.

"You know, you could always come by early," Lilian pushed, "maybe swing by the party?" There was a hopeless hope in her voice.

"That depends," Cas replied, "will your mother be bringing Cheese Dick?"

"Like... as an appetizer or...?" she responded dryly. He smirked back at her and she continued. "Yes, Father, she will be bringing her husband."

"Pass," he said bluntly. "Anyway, I've got that charity event Friday night so..."

"So you'll have to sleep off the booze and women?" she interrupted.

Cas put his hands up as though surrendering. "Your words."

Lilian shook her head, half amused, half annoyed. "Fine, you can come later, but don't go crazy on the gifts this year, ok? Please?"

"But how else am I going to be the favorite grandparent?" he asked innocently.

"Oh, I don't know," she began, "love and affection? Baseball games? Ice cream?"

"Baby Harley," he added.

"Only if you're looking to lose the favorite *parent* competition," she warned.

"Ouch," he said, putting his hand to his heart.

"Michael." She called into the other room. "He wanted to put his shoes on himself this time."

Cas laughed. That was his stubborn little man. Already trying to be independent. Just like Lilian had been at that age. It had been so difficult with her, letting her spread her wings and do things on her own. He'd tried not to be the helicopter dad, but he had always been extremely protective of her. Too much so. Her birth had been the single greatest moment of his life. His love for her, and now Michael, knew no bounds. They were his entire world. He was driven by this need to keep them close, safe. It didn't make any sense, his own childhood had been completely normal. There were no traumatic experiences to speak of that would justify his distrust of the world around him, but something in his bones always felt a threat present. Lurking somewhere, as though it were just waiting for the right moment to take what was most precious to him.

"Aaannd they're on backwards," Lilian said, setting the coat back down as Michael shuffled his way awkwardly into the room. His rumpled Lakers t-shirt, complete with chocolate ice cream stain, was stretched ever so slightly at the midsection and his little jeans bulged over his diaper. As he waddled in, he was looking down at his blue tennis shoes, toes pointing in the opposite direction.

"Mommy, look!" Michael shouted, proudly.

"I see!" she replied, picking him up.

Cas chuckled as he started adjusting Michael's shoes while she held him. "Good job, Buddy. I'm just going to make a few changes. Listen," he said quieter, fumbling with the Velcro, "I have a mission for you. I need you to kick your not-grandad in the nuts for me Saturday. Ok?"

"Dad!" Lilian snapped.

Cas stared at her for a moment, as if weighing his options while he pressed Michael's shoes back on, then looked back at him. "Chin is fine too."

"Dad." She used a warning tone this time.

"I'm compromising," Cas joked.

"Not funny," she said through a hint of a smile. She set Michael down and put his coat on.

"I'm a little funny," he defended himself.

"Alright, I'll give that to you. Tell Grandpa bye." She lifted Michael up again and leaned him into Cas for a kiss.

Cas squeezed him tightly and kissed his cheek. "Love you, Little Man. See you soon." Michael hugged him back and nodded his head yes. Cas kissed Lilian on the cheek as well.

"Bye, Daddy. Love you. See you Saturday," she said, grabbing her purse.

"Bye, Baby. Love you too. Drive careful," he replied, fighting off that old familiar feeling of danger, urging him to follow her out to the car and then to her house. She had started setting boundaries with him early on, evidently suffocated by his overprotective nature. Following her was definitely out of the question. He watched through the window as she put Michael in the car then got in and backed out of the driveway, then waited until her tail lights faded into the distance. The house was quiet.

Too quiet. But for those whispers, of course. He took another deep breath, then let his gaze wander, back up to the stars.

CHAPTER 15

Nikki tried to make himself as small as possible. He stood in the corner of Gordon's office hoping that nobody would ask him any important questions. Screw the hero dreams, he wanted nothing more than to be uninvolved in this as soon as possible. There were three other men in the room along with his boss. Two of them were military guys who looked pretty important. Nikki didn't know shit about the military, but there was an awful lot of hardware on the front of their uniforms. The third man wore a black suit and didn't say much so, naturally, he must be CIA and was most definitely there to kill him for seeing what he saw.

The four men had watched a recording of the satellite footage about six times, asked Nikki to go through the story twice, then immediately made phone calls. They were now quietly discussing the next steps. Gordon did more nodding than anything else, but would occasionally interject to provide more information on the satellite, it's location and the technology involved.

"How long?" one of the military men asked him.

"24 hours," Gordon responded. "And we won't be the only ones to have seen this so there's no point in delaying. It's probably best to get ahead of it and only release an image, not the video."

"Alright, we'll be in touch." They moved toward the office door. The man in black eyed Nikki as he followed the others through the door. Nikki swallowed hard, hoping he hadn't inadvertently pissed himself. He didn't move or speak, even after the door shut. Gordon sat behind his desk, removed his glasses and rubbed his face. Glancing up, he jumped slightly.

"Nikki, Jesus. I forgot you were there." He put his fingers to his temples, trying to ward off a headache.

"I don't know what to do," Nikki replied.

"Go back to your station," Gordon said with a hint of *'what the fuck do you think?'*

"Did you think they were going to kill you too?" Nikki asked before he could stop himself.

"What?" Gordon spat, clearly taken aback by the absurdity of the question.

"Nothing," Nikki said quickly, practically running from the office. He made his way down the corridor, checking his watch. Five hours left. Not even remotely religious, he found himself praying that nothing else would happen tonight that might get him disappeared.

CHAPTER 16

A young man in a blue suit stood waiting on the curb with a to-go coffee. Clean shaven and laser focused, you could practically smell his determination. He pulled out his phone and did a quick check for messages then returned it to his pocket, automatically straightening his posture as a small limousine came into view. After it pulled up, he reached down to open the door.

Cas stepped out, briefcase in his left hand while his right had a phone pressed to his ear. He wore his usual mild scowl and an expensive, gray suit that hugged all the right parts of his body. Handing the briefcase to the young man, he continued his conversation as they walked into the building. "Well, if he's not sure he can take his money to someone with the time to give a shit...... Yes, you can tell him I said that..... I'm not interested in his concerns, Dick..... because I'm smarter than he is and you can tell him I said that too. We've been over all of this. I don't play games. It's a go or no go. Call me back with his answer in a half hour."

The two of them got onto the elevator. Cas

put his phone away and took the coffee from the young man. "Thanks, Jack." He took a sip then touched his forehead, wincing in pain.

"Are you ok, Sir?" Jack asked.

"This damn headache," Cas said. "I don't think this day is going to help."

"I'll find you some aspirin," Jack volunteered.

"Thanks," Cas replied, "and maybe a sledge hammer."

They reached the top floor and exited the elevator. Cas walked straight into his office and closed the door. His office was enormous and sparce. Floor-to-ceiling windows served as his two outer walls and offered a breathtaking view. Inside sat a black, minimalist desk with a laptop and a single picture of Lilian and Michael, an L-shaped filing cabinet with a printer and paper shredder pushed into the corner, and a modern, black sofa facing a black, wall-mounted television. A single painting adorned the wall behind his desk; Starry Night, by Jean-François Millet. It was hard for Cas to describe how he felt about that particular painting, but, when asked why it was the only art he had in the room, he would always reply, "It makes me feel like I'm working from home."

Crossing the room, Cas grabbed the remote, flipped on the news, then walked with his coffee to look out at the world. The sun was still rising in the distance and the room was filled with orange light. Sipping his coffee he gazed up at the slowly lightening sky and took a deep breath. In the background he heard a female news anchor launch into a new story. "In breaking news, Nasa has reported a strange mass just outside the Earth's atmosphere." Cas turned quickly toward the TV as she continued, "They were able to capture a single photo before it knocked out satellite footage in the early hours of the morning." A photo popped up on the screen of what looked like pitch black dust or mist, blacking out the stars behind it. "So far, no one has been able to positively identify it, but one official states that this dust like accumulation is most likely the result of a deteriorated asteroid." Cas couldn't take his eyes off the screen, that photo. The hair on his neck stood up again, along with that feeling of dread. "One thing they could say for certain is that is poses no threat and, for now, remains a mystery." Still staring at the picture, the anchor's continuing comments were drowned out by the thudding of his heart. Something felt so incredibly wrong. Why did he feel like there was something he was supposed to be doing right now? What the fuck was wrong with him? His vision tunneled leaving only the image on the screen and an impulse to run, not away, but toward something. Pain suddenly shot through this head and he grabbed his temple. A knock at the door re-centered him.

"Yeah," he said.

The door opened and Jack came in carrying Cas's briefcase and a small, white bottle. "Sir, I found some aspirin."

"Thank God." Cas took the bottle. "No sledgehammer?" he asked, only half joking.

"Fresh out." Jack exaggerated a shrug and put the briefcase on Cas's desk.

"Thanks," Cas nodded.

"Yes Sir." Jack left the room, closing the door quietly behind him.

His cell phone started to ring in his pocket. Cas allowed himself one more glance at the sky before sitting at his desk and answering the call.

CHAPTER 17

"What the bloody hell is it?" Sadal asked. He hovered behind Shera along with Sal and Dorsum, watching the video on her laptop for the 7th time. Shera just shook her head in disbelief. This was exactly what she had seen in her dream and it scared the shit out of her. She had spent the last two days hoping that it wasn't real, trying to convince herself that maybe what she had seen had just been a symbol for something else, her brain turning a thing it couldn't understand into a sort of warped version of itself. She felt ill. Her heart was pounding and she was pretty sure her stomach was adjacent to her ankles. A familiar feeling of dread and inevitability crept up on her, taking form and leering at her from the dark corner of her mind.

"I have a theory," Sal began hesitantly, "but I'm not ... I didn't really consider it seriously until ... this." He gestured toward the laptop. "And believe me, you're not going to like it."

"That was sort of a given, wasn't it?" Shera grumbled. "Go on."

Standing up straight, his hand began to tap

on the table. He was clearly not anxious to share his theory, which was pretty unusual for him. Everyone, spread around Sadal's apartment again, had zeroed in on Sal. Ordinarily, he'd thrive on having the room's attention, but at the moment it seemed the last thing he wanted. "I think... I mean it could be ... it might be Nyx." Shera was pretty sure the entire room had stopped breathing. Nobody had been ready to hear what just came out of Sal's mouth. Including her. Part of her wanted to slap him for even saying the name or harshly brush him off and call the notion ridiculous. But she couldn't, because she knew in her gut he was right. Breaking the stillness in the room, she stood up and walked toward the kitchen, arms crossed and one hand supporting her chin. When she turned, her eyes went straight to Sadal. Meeting them with his own, he simply shook his head in denial.

"No," he insisted.

"Sadal," Sal urged, "it's the only thing that makes sense."

"None of this makes sense," Sadal shot back.

"He's right.," Shera interjected. "Sadal, he's right. It's her."

"How do you know?" he demanded.

"I know," Shera said matter-of-factly. It was enough. Sadal knew her well enough to understand that Shera wouldn't claim to be certain about something like this if she wasn't. He walked over to Porri who sat on the floor. Placing his back against the wall, he sank down next to her and took her hand.

Mina, who had been on the couch, got up to join Dorsum by the laptop. "It makes sense. Think about it, it makes sense."

Sal nodded. "The only one he's afraid of.... the only reason he'd allow us to..."

"So, what, you think he's hiding?" Shera interrupted, "And he's just *using* us to.."

"*He's* not going to face her," Sal interrupted back.

"He kept us alive for a suicide mission," Sadal mused quietly. Sal joined Nunki and sat on the arm of the chair next to her. Nobody spoke for a while, nobody knew what to say.

Shera leaned on the kitchen counter, facing away from the others. This couldn't be happening. Her thoughts wandered to Cas and Lilian. They would have no idea. *The whole world has no idea what was coming.* Trying to control her imagination, she couldn't fight off the images of fire or stop the sound of people screaming in her head. "Why would she come here? What possible reason could she have for coming here now?" No one had an answer.

Brach clapped his hands together. "Well, looks like we don't have much of a choice. We're going to have to do this and do it without his help."

"If he's going to be a pussy about it, yeah," Shera seethed. She sat on the counter stool. "Do you think she knows about us?"

"I thought about that too," Sal agreed. "I think that's why she stopped where she did."

"Maybe that's a good thing," Nunki added, hopefully. "Maybe that means we're a threat?"

Sadal, looking a little less dejected, kissed Porri's hand. "Maybe. Not separately, but together. There could be a chance. All of us. Together."

"Always a catch," Les chimed in. "Guess that means we need to stick around for a while."

"It does. And nobody goes anywhere without their half," Sadal answered.

Les laughed. There was little chance of that happening. His and Maia's arms were intertwined. They looked at one another and smiled. "Evidently we need to make the most of the time."

"Let's call it a night," Sadal offered. "We'll figure out the next step tomorrow."

Everyone stood and started prepping to leave. They were all staying in separate places at the moment. Most had rented rooms at nearby hotels, but that was going to have to change. They were going to need to move to another location where they could all be under the same roof. Shera was pretty sure they were all thinking of the same place, too. She pulled Sadal aside, "I have to go." He looked as though he was going to argue, but she stopped him. "No objections. You know I have to. If we're really a threat, she'll go after him."

"Assuming, she does know about us, and where to find us," Sadal said with a hand up to show he wasn't going to fight her, "what do you think she would do?"

"I have no idea," Shera admitted. "Kill him. Break him. Use his family. Point is, he's the only one who is vulnerable right now."

"Not the only one." Sadal reminded her. "I won't stop you..... when you need us..."

"I'll call you." Shera grabbed his shoulder reassuringly. He pulled her in and hugged her tightly. Shera didn't know what lay ahead, but the thought of facing it without her friend there made her more uneasy. And the thought of not being there if they needed her was even worse. She didn't see any other options, though. Cas was alone and completely blind to what was coming, if she had to die to keep him and Lilian safe then that's what she would do. Porri came over and kissed her on the cheek, not having to ask what was going on.

"Be careful." She whispered.

Shera nodded, trying to keep her emotions in check, then turned and walked quickly out the door. Hopefully, she could catch a flight today.

CHAPTER 18

The house was peaceful. Lilian leaned slightly against the sink while she scrubbed the pan, keeping half of her attention on the other room. She heard Bob the Builder droning on in his usual overly cheerful voice and knew that Michael would be dutifully glued to the television while Alison was in her post dinner coma on the sofa. The kitchen was dimly lit by only the under-cabinet and the sink lights, but it was plenty to wash by. Besides, it gave Lilian a better view of the back yard, which she loved to look out at while she was in here. Alison had insisted they remodel this section of the house before they moved in. She knew that Lilian was in love with the yard, and since she spent so much time in the kitchen, she'd thought it would make her happy to combine the two as much as possible. Alison was right, it was perfect. From her giant three-pane convex window Lillian could see every inch of her paradise. The hedge just high enough to make the home seem devoid of neighbors. There was a vegetable garden and a greenhouse to the left tucked in with a little white picket fence. On the right, just beyond the patio, a small pool and a river of flowers lined the hedges. Perfect.

Lilian smiled to herself as she rinsed the pan then jumped. Had she just seen something out there? It was dark, but she could still see most of the yard. She searched the area where she thought something had moved, but nothing. Maybe it was a bird, or her imagination. Shrugging it off, she went back to the dishes when something, a shadow, appeared then disappeared just as quickly. This time she knew she'd seen something. "Alison," she called as quietly as she could, but loud enough for her to hear. She must have heard the nervousness in Lilian's voice because, instead of calling back from the other room, which she would normally have done, her figure was almost instantly in the doorway.

"What's up, Babe?" Lilian didn't answer. She was as still as a statue in front of the window. "Honey?" Alison continued, concerned. "What's wrong? Are you ok?"

A chilling noise between a screech and a scream drifted in from the backyard. Lilian looked at Alison, obviously terrified. "Did you hear that?" she gasped. Alison was in instant protection mode. She pointed toward the other room, directing Lilian to go there while she walked toward the door to the backyard. Opening it slowly, she inched outside. It had to be an animal of some kind; what else would make that noise? Realizing she had nothing to defend herself with, she desperately looked around. The baseball bat and mitt she'd been using earlier with Michael were, thankfully, still there. She quickly grabbed the bat and moved a bit further out onto the patio. Having ignored her instructions to go into the other room, Lilian followed her and now stood in the open doorway. "Do you see anything?" she whispered loudly.

Alison shook her head. "Nothing," she said back, then froze. A creature suddenly appeared in front of the hedge. At first, all Alison could see was the eyes. Less like eyes and more like lanterns, lit with a moving flame. As it moved forward and stopped to watch her, it had become illuminated enough to see clearly. Her blood turned to ice. It had to be 7 feet tall or more. It was a man, but not a man; more of a skeleton with patches of flesh and wings. Alison's brain instantly darted back to nightmares she'd had about the Moth Man as a child. Blinking her eyes quickly, she half expected it to vanish. It couldn't be real. Behind her, Lilian gasped. They were both frozen in absolute terror. The creature looked like it was on fire, burning from the inside out, surrounded by a thick, black, swirling smoke. The worst part were its eyes. There was more than just fire there, they were scorched with rage. Pure, blinding rage, hate, agony. Alison was unable to move or breathe, that is until it started toward her and reality came crashing down. "Oh my God," she cried, turning toward the door and seeing Lilian there. "Lil, go! Get Mika!" She looked back toward the creature and stumbled, landing hard on her tailbone. Her eyes shot up in time to see the thing not more than a couple feet away. She could feel the heat coming off of it and smell the odor like burning garbage. Hearing Lilian scream behind her and thinking she wouldn't have time to get away she yelled, "Run!" Clenching her jaw, Alison prepared herself for the worst.

Unexpectedly, the thing was no longer in front of her. Another shadow had flown in from her left and both were now tumbling across the lawn. The other figure, much smaller, was a woman. She wore some kind of armor that reflected the moonlight like water. The woman got to her feet, holding a sword in front of her and a shield on her arm. A green gem shone brightly from her chest and another from the hilt of her blade. She was dwarfed by the creature, but seemed not to notice. The creature screamed loudly and Alison covered her ears. This couldn't be happening. Lilian's arms flew around her, dragging her back toward the house, but neither of them made it inside. They halted in the doorway, unable to look away from the yard. The skeleton launched at the woman. She dodged right, throwing her sword upward and severing the creatures left wing. Shrieking in pain, it reached out and grabbed her around the neck, lifting her upward. Without hesitation, she threw her left leg up around its arm and pulled her body over it, forcing it to bend at the elbow. She then pulled both ends of her sword toward her chest, cutting its hand off at the wrist. Another horrible scream followed while she fell to the ground and rolled to her feet. Again, it lunged. This time she fell to her knees and shoved her sword upward through its chest. Withdrawing it, she turned toward the fence that surrounded the pool and ran up it. Reaching the top she pushed off hard with her legs and spun, swinging her sword along with her, catching the creature's neck as she turned. Its head flew off and it fell to the ground, instantly evaporating into ash and dying flame.

For what felt like an eternity, the yard was quiet and nobody moved. At last, the woman looked up at Alison and Lilian. Walking swiftly toward the house, she pointed her sword at the doorway, "Get inside," she instructed. Alison obediently turned. Lilian backed into the house, followed by Alison and the woman.

"What the hell was that?" Alison blurted out as they entered. "Who are you?"

"We don't have time for me to explain. My name is Shera. That'll have to be enough for now." She closed the door and scanned the yard through the glass. "Lilian, I need you to listen to me."

"Do I know you?" Lilian asked, bewildered.

"No. Stop talking and listen. I hate to sound cliché, but you know that part in the movies where they say, 'come with me if you want to live'?" Shera hinted. "This is that part. Get Michael and some clothes. We're leaving."

"What? Why?" Alison blurted.

"Well, I can sit here and explain it to you and give five more of those things time to show up, or you can get your shit and we can leave before they do," Shera asserted. She hated herself for sounding so harsh, but they needed to hurry.

Without another word, Alison and Lilian exchange looks then left the room to collect Michael and their things. Shera took a breath, her armor appearing to disintegrate around her as she reached for her phone. Never in her life did she think she'd actually be in this house. And when she had dreamed about it, it certainly wasn't under these circumstances. She dialed Sadal. "Shera?" his voice came through the other end after it had barely begun to ring.

"I was right. She went after his family."

"Are you... are they.." he started

"We're fine," she promised. "What's more,

I got up close and personal with what we're facing."

"With her?"

"No... with one of her flying monkeys."

" .... bad?" he asked, not sounding like he wanted to know the answer.

"Well..... there's a smell." Shera knew she wouldn't be able to go into too much detail right now. "It was just one, this time. How soon can you get everyone here?"

"We're at the temple, Shera." Shera grinned, she should have known he'd be a step ahead of her. Sadal was a fucking diamond. It had been a long, long time since she had been to the temple. But it was still hidden, and safe enough for Lilian. It wasn't too far either, about a nine hour drive.

"You're a good man, Sadal," she said earnestly. "Get ready, I'm bringing them to you." Hanging up the phone she closed her eyes and let her head fall. "Cas," she whispered to herself, hoping against hope that some part of him could still hear her, "please be careful." She looked up as Alison scuffled into the room with two bags, followed by Lilian with a bag and Michael. They stopped abruptly when they saw her. For a second she didn't know what the issue was, then realized.

"Your... clothes..." Alison stammered, confused.

"The armor is there when I need it," Shera said, urging them out the door. "We're taking my car." She hurried them down to her old Ford Bronco and tossed the bags in while Alison set up Michael's car seat. Lilian got into the passenger seat while Alison sat in the back trying to sooth an out-of-sorts toddler. Shera cranked the engine and slammed it into gear. *Let's just hope they don't try to catch us on the road*, she thought.

CHAPTER 19

Cas stood at his bar alone, a bottle of Domaine Leroy Musigny Grand Cru in front of him. He'd needed a pick me up after today. Or, rather, something to calm him down. He swirled the pinot noir in his glass then emersed his nose beneath the rim. Intoxicating. Holding his eyes shut, he took a sip and let it sit in his mouth. That first sip was always the best. Subtle and exquisite. He set the glass down, took a deep breath then let it out and closed his eyes. He needed this.

Without warning, a sense hit him like a punch to the gut. He thought he was alone. He was wrong. His eyes shot open. In the bar's mirrored backsplash he could see a shadow at the back of the room. *Who the fuck ...?* His hair stood on end and his muscles tightened, but he didn't move. He would have expected to have felt fear at a time like this, but surprisingly, what he felt more than anything was overwhelming anger. He could hear his heart pounding in an unusual rhythm, almost like it was (strange as it was) chanting. Heat began rising up through his spine, turning his face and his vision red. He didn't know what was behind him, but he knew for certain he wanted to kill it. Just then he heard growling, like last night, but much clearer. It was slow, guttural, and so loud it rocked the room. He clenched his jaw as pain cracked through his head like lightning. Reaching down, he gripped the lip of the bar's marble countertop. He could see the reflection of the shadow still behind him begin to shrink toward the ground. *What is it doing?* It was crouching. *It's getting ready to pounce.* He gripped the bar tighter and glared at it. He felt an energy like he'd never felt coming to the surface, bursting through his skin, an emotion he couldn't even begin to describe, blinding power. *Turn around*, he thought to himself. Suddenly the world flashed white. Then dark. Then silent.

He blinked. The shadow's reflection was gone. The room was empty again. He turned to make sure he was alone then looked down at his hand. He held a massive piece of the bar in his still clenched fist. "Jesus," he said aloud. *What the hell had just happened*? Setting the chunk of marble down, he backed up until his legs hit the couch then sat, disorientated. Any hint of negativity that had been in the room had utterly vanished. Had he just ... did he imagine that? "Fuck," he groaned aloud again. "Do I need a doctor or a fucking priest?" he asked the empty room, then leaned back and covered his head with his hands.

CHAPTER 20

Shera let the air out of her mouth slowly, trying to be quiet. She was shaking and sweating. Seeing her abnormally white hands, she relaxed her grip on the steering wheel feeling the blood rush back into them. *Fuck*, she thought, *fuck was close.* She wasn't certain what had happened, but she knew he needed help. One minute she was fine and the next she felt like she'd been punched in the stomach. Then, she'd seen his face. Shera didn't have to see or hear Nyx to know she'd been in the room with him, or a part of her at least. She had chanted, barely audible, sending him her energy, hoping that he could hear her and take it. Her head filled with light and noise and then... nothing. It was over. He was alive and Nyx was gone. Beyond that, she knew nothing. She glanced sideways and saw Lilian staring at her. It's no wonder, she was sure she looked like a crazy person.

They'd been out of the city for a long time. All you could see, aside from the occasional car, was a bit of road lit by the headlights and a hint of what lay beyond in the otherwise vast darkness. Any other day Shera would have thought little of it, but on this particular night she found it unnerving. No doubt, by her tense posture, Lilian was of the same mindset. Unbelievable, how many times had she imagined herself having a conversation with this girl and now ...any words they may have exchanged in that fantasy seemed entirely irrelevant. Well, there was no point in avoiding it now. Lilian was going to expect answers eventually. Whether she sounded like a whackjob now or later, Shera would need to give them to her. "You haven't asked me any questions yet," she said softly, careful not to wake Alison or Michael who were passed out in the back. "I thought for sure I would get bombarded as soon as we got in the car."

"Honestly," Lilian replied, "I don't know where to start."

"That makes two of us," admitted Shera.

"That thing...at the house...I... what..?" Lilian struggled to find the words.

"Let me help you," Shera offered. "That thing was what you would probably refer to as a demon. Or a soldier. Your choice."

"Demon?" Lilian said shrilly. "Like .... demon

from hell? Yeah, try again. I don't believe in that crap."

"Yes and no," Shera said. "Hell in a matter of speaking, but not really in the sense you're referring to."

"Enlighten me," Lilian pushed.

Shera sighed. *Here we go, this is where she assumes I just got out of the loony bin.* "I'll do my best, but you're going to have to open your mind to some possibilities you may not have accepted before. Considering what you just saw.... Okay, you know what the underworld is?"

"Yeah, me and every kid who watched The Mummy," Lilian spat.

Shera kept her voice calm. Lilian was using sarcasm to cope and she couldn't blame her. The scope of this girl's reality was about to change drastically in a very short period of time. She was allowed her mechanisms. "Greek mythology underworld, not Hollywood."

"Not really, no," Lilian admitted.

"Okay, for the sake of simplicity let's just think of the underworld less like a place and more like a... I don't know... state of mind. Or like something that *any* place can be turned into for anyone," Shera struggled through the explanation.

"Alright, I don't like where *this* is going." Lilian retorted.

"No, you won't," Shera said honestly. "There is a... not a person, but an entity or... being, whatever you want to call her."

"Her?" Lilian questioned.

Shera nodded. "Her. Yes. Her name is Nyx."

"I'm not following," Lilian spat again.

"That's because I'm doing a really shit job of explaining it," Shera grumbled. "Look, I know it sounds crazy. I know I sound certifiable, but all of those things that you thought were just stories are not... those mythological figures they taught you about in school.... they're not myths. Nyx is not a myth. She is very real. She is very dangerous. And she is very much here. "

"To do what?"

"I can only assume to turn Earth into another underworld. Que the scoffing."

"I'm not scoffing," Lilian said seriously. "I mean I might have before that thing attacked Alison. I don't understand how. How is what you're saying even possible? I mean aside from the fact that the notion sounds ridiculous, how could you turn an entire planet into an underworld?"

"Well, Nyx has children, many children," Shera explained, "Moros, Ker, Thanatos, Momus, Oizys, Apate, Eris, the list goes on. They are what you would think of as sort of a living essence of the worst things imaginable. Doom, destruction, death, pain, deceit , strife... you name it. Picture the most negative energy you can, the worst flaws of humanity, as its own kind of consciousness, taking its own form. Those are her children. Her generals, so to speak. Nyx will... unleash her children on the world, and, under their control, her army of demons, one of which you had the pleasure of meeting tonight."

"Jesus," Lilian whispered, "unleash them to what, kill us?"

"No, no. It's much worse than death. Death is too easy, too kind. Nyx wants you to suffer. They will possess every living thing on the plane."

"Possess?" Lilian looked terrified.

"Yes. They will take one soul at a time and remove everything but pain, hatred and despair. Make us prisoners in our own minds and let us writhe there for eternity. Lilian, I know this sounds like some shit a doomsday yahoo would be spouting out on a street corner, but I cannot possibly convey how serious this is. Everything good in this world is about to disappear, because humanity will lose all ability to see it. Your wife, your child." Shera nodded to the back seat. "They won't be there anymore. Just a shell of who they were. In a living nightmare."

For a long while the two of them sat in silence. Lilian didn't know how to respond and Shera didn't know how to ease her or how to apologize for bluntly ruining her life. Maybe she should have phrased it differently? No, Lilian was stronger than she realized. This was the right way to tell her.

"I think I need to call my dad," Lilian said finally, as if reading Shera's mind.

"Your father is safe for now," Shera replied. Wanting to stop the conversation there.

"How do you know that?" Lilian demanded.

"I just know," Shera said shortly. "You can't tell him anything right now. Trust me."

"Trust you?" Lilian cried, "I don't know you. .. I'm sorry.. I know that sounded... I'm not ungrateful. I'm just.... I mean, I don't understand, why were *we* attacked? How many other people?"

Shera knew where this was going and wasn't anxious to continue. She hesitated, "None."

"None?" Lilian said slowly. "You're saying we were the only ones? Please tell me that is just a coincidence." Shera's silence was all the response she needed. "Why? Why us?"

Shera sighed. "I'm sorry, Lilian, I can't answer that."

"Can't?" Lilian pried. "Or won't?"

Shera got quiet again. After a moment she looked back at Lilian. "Both. You should probably try to get some sleep. We won't be there until morning."

Lilian just glared at her for a few minutes then turned to look out the window. Shera tried to push the heartache down. There was just no easy way to do this. She could practically feel how much this girl hated her, having no idea how much Shera actually loved her. *Figures.*

The drive went by slowly. Eventually Lilian drifted off to sleep, leaving Shera in her thoughts. It was difficult to concentrate on the road or keep her head in the game knowing that Cas could be in serious danger at any moment. She couldn't get his face out of her mind, his heartbeat pounding in her ears. Shaking off the exhaustion, she told herself that the sooner she got Lil and her family to the temple, the sooner she could go back and keep an eye on him. Of course, she had absolutely no idea what she would do if he needed her. She couldn't tell him the truth. Certainly not about them or even himself. There were no good options, just an impending shitstorm.

CHAPTER 21

The intercom on his desk buzzed loudly, "Sir?" Jacks voice came through.

"Go ahead." Cas wasn't able to sleep after last night so he had dragged Jack in early. *Poor kid*, Cas thought, he was worth his weight in gold, though. Never complained, never called in, just worked his ass off. He had earned his bonus this year, that was for sure.

"Your ex-wife is on line one," Cas looked at the intercom. He couldn't see Jack's face, but Cas knew he'd been wincing when he announced the caller. *Jesus, what the fuck is Andrea calling me for at this hour? The fucking sun isn't even up.*

"Sir?" Jack said again after a few seconds. "Did you want me to put her through?"

"A window, maybe," Cas muttered.

"Sir, I apologize, I didn't hear that," Jack pleaded in his 'don't kill the messenger' voice.

"Put her through, Jack," Cas said reluctantly.

"Yes, Sir." Jack turned off the intercom and transferred the call. Looking down at the blinking light, Cas considered hanging up on her. He got up, pressed the speaker button, then began pacing.

"Hello, Andrea," he grumbled.

"Castor." Andrea's sing song way of saying his name made him cringe. It was like nails on a chalkboard. Were it not for the gift of his daughter and grandson, Cas would have regretted ever meeting Andrea. It's not that he didn't believe in love, but he certainly didn't believe it was something he would ever find. He had this vision in his mind of the perfect woman and, somehow, every other women fell short. At a certain point in his life he just gave up on the idea, choosing to focus on how they looked in a tight dress while climbing out of an expensive car. He was a young idiot and he had paid for it. She was a bombshell and a trophy which she both knew and wanted. At no point had there ever been love between them. "I want to know if you plan on going this weekend," she continued.

Seriously? Cas was dumfounded. "That's why you're calling? Andie, it's five in the morning."

"Well, you're up, aren't you?" she retorted.

Cas sighed. "No, I told Lilian no." There was a

brief silence in which he imagined her fuming, that, at least, brightened his mood a bit.

"You're going to have to get used to him eventually," she said finally.

"No, I really don't," he disagreed. This was really the last thing he needed right now, a demanding ex-wife. Why was it so dammed important to her that he like her new sucker squeeze? The guy had the social skills of a serial killer and business sense of a cracker jack. Yet he was pompous enough to believe in his own superiority over the rest of mankind. Always wanting to debate over topics he was no authority on and had nothing but secondhand fallacies to back up. He dealt with a lot of people like this over the years, but he always had the option of telling them to fuck off. This particular one kept coming back, like a bad breakfast. "You're the one who married him, why are you asking me to play house?"

"You don't have to be pissed at him just because I got remarried," she hissed back through the speaker.

"Pissed?" he exclaimed. "I'm not pissed at him for that. If anything he did me a favor, but that doesn't mean I have to like the guy. He's a schmuck."

"Oh, so this isn't just you harboring regrets and taking it out on him?" she pushed him.

"Don't psychoanalyze me, Andie. If that's the shit you're shrink is telling you then I promise you, you're paying her too much. I don't have any regrets about the way it ended. You left me, not the other way around, and I am much better off." He was beginning to feel his temperature rise.

"I walked out, Cas, but you left me a long time ago," she kept going. "You spent all your time looking out that stupid window and playing with your telescope. We never did anything or went anywhere, but you were never happy where you were."

Cas let his head fall then sat down in his chair. She wasn't wrong, not there at least. "Andrea, please, I really don't want to do this right now." He must have sounded more exhausted than he realized, because she relented.

After a few seconds of silence she came through again. "Ok, I apologize. I just... I would appreciate it if you'd try and make an effort with Danny, okay?"

"Okay," he said, grudgingly, "I promise the next time I see him I'll make an effort."

"That's all I wanted," she said almost gleefully. "Thank you. Because you're probably going to see us on Friday. We're going to the charity auction."

Cas's head hit the desk. He had actually not been looking forward to the event already and now …… lifting his head up, he searched his mind for a response that would not launch them into another argument and came up with nothing. At last he settled on, "I'm going to hang up now." He reached his hand over to the phone and hit the red button just as she had started to say something else. Her voice blissfully disappeared. He clenched his fist then hit the intercom button. "Jack."

"Yes, Sir?" Jack responded immediately.

"I'm going to need more aspirin," Cas said.

"I'll get it now, Sir." The intercom clicked off. Cas rested his head on the desk for another minute then got up again and walked to the window. The sun was just starting to come up, bathing his face in a dull, orange light. He allowed himself to get lost in it. Staring into the distance he recalled a moment from last night. In the deepest parts of his mind he could still hear it. Chanting. Chanting in a voice that, for some inexplicable reason, haunted his very core.

CHAPTER 22

"Bullshit!" Sal exclaimed.

"True story," Dorsum swore, holding his hands up as if to signify his innocence and trustworthiness.

"Bullshit!" Sal repeated.

"Like a bear." Dorsum's hands had now moved to his sides, arms extended out wide to demonstrate the size of his foe.

"What's going on?" Maia asked as she and Les entered the room, each gripping a mug of steaming coffee. They stepped down into the sunken seating area and claimed a large, red cushion, him sitting first, then her, nestling up against him. The gray stone room was both softened and brightened by the addition of a red rug and colorful seating cushions for them to lounge on during breaks. They all sat together. Well, all but Porri who was in the kitchen, and Sadal who was prepping the sleeping quarters for their guests.

Sal was shaking his head no as he looked at Maia, "Dors has invented some wild fiction.."

"Not a fiction!" Dorsum insisted.

"..wild fiction," Sal continued, " in which he claims to have fought the Erymanthian Boar."

Maia and Les both laughed while Dorsum continued to mutter "..not a fiction.."

"So, this would be *before* Hercules then," Brach teased, leaning back against a yellow cushion smiling, arm in arm with Resha.

"And, obviously, you lost, right?" Resha added.

Dorsum hesitated, looking as though he was navigating his way through the answer in his brain. "Well," he admitted finally, "... maybe... it wasn't so much a fight as..."

"I knew it!" Sal yelled. Nunki, beside him, put her hand to her stomach and doubled over, her body convulsing in silent hysterics.

"It was big," Dorsum relented.

Mina took his hand and patted it. "I still think you're brave." She winked at him and he blushed, causing another round of laughter from the group. None of them could remember the last time they'd felt this happy. Or at least it was a time they'd all tried to push away, having had no hopes of ever being together again, ever feeling this sort of love and closeness.

There was so much joy in that moment it was almost painful. Closer than friends or family. Closer than anyone could comprehend. When the laughter died down, they all sat quietly for a moment looking at one another and thinking the same thing. The awareness that their happiness would be short lived creeping back in, taking hold. Knowing that, even if they all survived, separation would inevitably follow. Why could they not force this moment to last for an eternity?

The silence was broken when Sadal entered from the hallway. "They should be here soon," he said.

"I wonder if they look like him," Maia thought aloud.

Nunki smiled and tugged on Sal's ear. "A baby," she mused, "can you imagine?" Sal took her hand and smiled back.

CHAPTER 23

Shera rolled the window down and pointed her face toward the orange glow. The sun had started to rise. Letting the cool breeze touch her skin, the light embraced her, lifting her upwards even as thoughts of Cas weighed her down. The front tire hit a hole in the road and jolted the Bronco's passengers awake. Lilian looked around quickly as though she didn't recognize where she was. Shera watched memory, reality and resignation take their turns with her and decided it would be best to wait for her to speak. They drove for another few minutes, Lilian and Alison taking in their surroundings. The road they were on, if you could call it that, was not paved. It was more of a hiking path that was big enough to drive your car over. A large field spread out to their left and a thick, wooded forest lay in every other direction.

"Where are we?" Lilian asked. You could tell that part of her didn't actually want to know. It would just be another nail in the coffin of her previously perfect life.

"A safe place," Shera assured her.

"Safe from what? More of those things?" Alison asked through a yawn in the back. Both Shera and Lilian looked at her then at each other. She hadn't been awake for their conversation last night.

"I guess I'll be catching her up," Lilian said quietly.

It was everything Shera could do not to take her hand. She wanted to apologize to her, to tell her everything was going to be okay and that as long as she was alive she wouldn't let anything happen to them. But she couldn't. She wanted to tell her things would go back to normal. But she couldn't. She wanted to tell her she loved her. But...."Were almost there."

A shape was now visible at the far end of the field. It looked like a small house or building. As they got closer, Lilian and Alison strained to get a better view. It was actually larger than it appeared to be before. "It's a compound," Alison said.

"It's a temple," corrected Shera. "It's our temple." As they pulled up, the true age of the structure began to show. The rock exterior was crumbling in several places and nearly every wall was almost entirely taken over by ivy. There were steps leading up to a platform and giant, wooden double doors. Sadal waited on the platform for them to stop the car.

"Who is that?" Lilian asked

"He's one of the people here to protect you." Shera shut off the car and climbed out. Lilian followed her. Sadal had come down the steps and walked toward them. He took Shera by the shoulders and kissed her forehead. The expression on his face, a mix of relief and concern, confused Lilian. He turned toward her and Alison and smiled warmly.

"Hello, I'm Sadal. Welcome to the temple. Don't worry, it looks much better on the inside." He took their hands and was instantly disarming. Both Lilian and Alison relaxed a little. Shera walked around to get the bags while Porri came out to greet them.

"Oh, my," she said, taking Lilian's hands tightly, her eyes lighting up. "You all must be exhausted. I'm so sorry for what you've been through. Please come inside." Both she and Sadal were beaming at Lilian, which caught her a little off guard. She saw Shera getting the bags and went to grab one while Alison got Michael.

"Who are the people here?" Lilian whispered to Shera.

Hesitating, Shera furrowed her brow. "You remember me telling you that Nyx has an army?"

Lilian nodded.

"Well," Shera continued, "so do we. A bit smaller, I'll grant you."

Lilian glanced back over at Sadal and Porri who looked like they just had the wind taken out of them. They were holding hands and their eyes were glued to Michael. There was no threat in their eyes, but the same sort of affection she'd seen when they took her hands. "Why do they look that way at us?"

"I'm probably not the best person to tell you that." Shera said, starting to walk past her. "Come on." Shera walked up the steps and pushed the massive doors open. Lilian entered behind her, followed by Alison holding Michael. Sadal and Porri came in last and shut the doors, sliding a thick plank down to lock it. Shera smiled, just as she'd remembered. The large room had statues and inlays lining the walls, which, along with the floors, were made entirely of gray stone. The center of the room was a sunken rectangle with steps encasing it. The sunken portion was home to a rug and several cushions for resting and meditation; as well as, at the moment, the rest of their little gathering. Four massive, stone pillars helped to support the weight of the roof. Just beyond the entry room was a large opening to the kitchen and a view of the training courtyard, and to the left there was a hallway entrance where all of the sleeping quarters could be found. Shera took a deep breath in. She had missed this place.

Sadal cleared his throat to make the introductions. "This is Mina, Sal, Resha, Brach, Nunki, Les, and Maia. Of course, you already met Porri." Everyone stood and came closer as Sadal gestured to their guests. "Guys, this is Lilian,

Alison, and little Michael." There was a bit of an awkward silence while the group stared.

Brach touched Shera's elbow. "This is..."

"Yes," she responded before he could finish.

"Cas," he gasped, looking as though he didn't know what to feel.

"Yes," Shera said again. Noticing that Lilian had heard him say her father's name.

Then they were practically rushed. Nunki and Mina were gushing over Michael and not knowing what to make of it, Alison just let them. Shera watched them with him for as long as she could take then set the bag she'd been carrying down. She could feel all the pain she'd been pushing down rising to the surface. A century of unwept tears. Her hands shaking, she tried to steady her voice. Not wanting to lose her composure. "Porri, would you mind taking care of them? I need to clean up." Not waiting for an answer, Shera walked as fast as she could from the room.

Lilian saw Porri's face in time to catch the heartbreak as she stared after Shera. "Of course." Catching Lilian's gaze, she smiled again. "Let's get you settled in. You must be hungry too."

"Alright," Sadal clapped his hands together. "Breaks over. Let's get back to it." A general groan filled the room as they all slowly started making their way to the courtyard. Alison's hand shot out to grab Lilian's arm when she saw what looked like beams of light shooting out from each person, leaving in its place armor where there had been none, just like they'd seen on Shera.

"What the ...?" escaped from Alison's mouth.

Porri glanced at Lilian who shrugged and shook her head. "She was asleep."

Porri nodded, walked over to Alison and put an arm around her shoulder, guiding her toward the kitchen. "So I take it you haven't heard," she began. "Let's get you fed. It's going to be a long morning."

CHAPTER 24

Shera closed the door, dropped her go bag, slid her jacket off and examined the room. Just as she'd remembered it. Cold, stone, characterless and damp. Three hundred years worth of morning dew left a musty smell in the air. There was a bed with a new mattress, freshly made (no doubt Sadal's doing), a single wooden chair with a clean towel draped over it, and a wardrobe. In the corner was a shower tub and sink underneath a small, wall mounted mirror. Morning light poured in through a large window, tiny dust particles dancing in its beam. No creature comforts to speak of, but it felt like home. Tossing her jacket on the bed she walked to the window. Not a cloud in the sky. *Of course*, she thought, *that's about to change.* She lifted her hand and pressed it to the glass, closing her eyes, trying to feel the energy of the sun. But it was useless, all she could feel was Cas. He was all she felt, all she thought of, all she wanted. She couldn't shake him.

Unbeknownst to her, on the top floor of his building, Cas stood at his usual place by the window, looking out. An urge to place his hand against the glass overtook him. Putting his palm to the sun, his chest heaved as he felt his body fill with emotions that didn't make any sense to him. His heart was yearning, reaching out for something that wasn't there. So close to touching it, as though it was reaching back. Like all he had to do was fold his fingers forward and they would be intertwined with another's.

Shera's heart was pounding and the room, spinning. She felt his palm on hers, felt his pulse, his rough fingertips, his heat. Then, with a wave of emotion, she slammed her fist into the glass, shattering it.

Cas brought his hand back, pain shooting through it, as though it had just been sliced open. Seeing no wound, he massaged it. Disorienting confusion filling the void that had moments before been something inexplicable.

Stumbling over to the sink, Shera leaned on it, trying to steady herself. "Stop. He's gone." She had spent a century and a half writhing under the torment of losing him. Emptying each existence of its tears. It took every fiber of her strength to accept that he had been lost to her and that she would have to face eternity with not only no hope of his touch, but without the comfort of knowing that, wherever he was, he loved her as she did him. She couldn't.... she could not allow herself even a glimmer of hope now. He was her universe, the other half of her soul, the only thing that could complete her, and he was gone. She felt as though she was going to vomit. Trying to slow her breathing and gripping the sink as tightly as she could, she knew she was not going to win the fight this time. Suffering washed over her and she collapsed to the floor, weeping. Grief, loneliness and utter despair were her only companions in this moment. His face burned in her mind as she drowned in loss.

CHAPTER 25

Lilian and Alison sat at the small kitchen table. The room looked like something out of a renaissance movie. No modern amenities. A fireplace for a stove, a brick oven, and prep space that looked more like a medieval altar than a kitchen island. Still, Porri seemed to be making it work. There was fresh baked bread, hot soup, and roasted chicken. Enough to feed an army, fittingly. The hand carved table they dined at was, no doubt, older than Lilian and Alison combined. A large opening before them allowed a full view of the courtyard, peppering their conversation with clangs of metal, grunts and laughter. Michael lay on a blanket nearby watching one of his shows on Alison's iPad.

Alison was lost in thought. She'd just been caught up on the situation and was taking it as well as could be expected. Robotically chomping on some bread, she watched the courtyard sparring while Lilian rubbed her hand over Alison's back. Putting her elbow on the table and resting her chin, she glanced back at Michael.

"He's so beautiful," Porri said softly. "I honestly never thought I'd see it."

"See what?" Lilian asked, "A baby?"

"He's a special baby," Porri came back.

"Why?" pressed Lilian.

Porri took a breath. "I'm not sure it's my place to tell you."

"Everyone keeps saying that," Lilian scoffed, losing her patience. "What are you people not telling us? Why is my baby 'special'? Why does everyone keep looking at us like they know us? Why did that man say my dad's name earlier? What are *we doing* here?" Lilian paused, trying to calm and lower her voice. "Please." She pleaded, "please tell me the truth. It can't be any worse than what we've already heard."

Alison had come back to her senses and now turned her attention to Porri as well. Porri remained quiet for a minute, debating with herself, then seemed to decide. "Alright. Where to start?" She sat at the table with them. "Do you know Plato at all?"

"Sure, I guess," Lilian replied. "But I'm not... I mean, I read him in school."

Porri, thinking they were off to a bad start

looked toward the courtyard. "Sadal is really the best one to tell you about this."

"Please," Lilian pleaded again, taking her hand.

Porri lowered her head, gathered her thoughts, then continued. "There was a man named Aristophanes who Plato wrote about. He had a theory that all of the world's first humans were actually what you would think of as two people, conjoined. Whole, as they were mean to be, each person was more powerful than you could imagine. Try to picture massive beings, immortal, strong enough to crush mountains, that can shine as brightly as the sun." Porri paused to make sure they were keeping up. "Well, in this theory, the Greek god Zeus began to worry about these people, because in numbers they were too powerful for him to control. So, to make sure he remained in power, he split them in two, sending them to opposite ends of the world and making sure they spent every lifetime just searching for one another."

"Okay...that's... awful, but..." Lilian started, "I don't really understand. Are you telling me that's not a myth either?"

"In part, no. It just wasn't every human. In fact, there were only six of us and we weren't exactly human. There weren't any humans, yet. We... were beings, stars. We each had a unique gravitational field that held us together at exactly the right distance from each other, drawn to a center. Imagine five stars in a circle rotating around a single, larger star. That was us. Our energy was connected. The six of us together were creating one singularly powerful energy. I don't know that it's possible for you to conceive of it. The human mind is molded to fit into a certain concept of what is or isn't possible, but reality is... so much more magical than you realize. Anyway, Zeus saw what we were becoming, and took it as a threat. First, he shattered the circle, then split each star in two and sent them to separate constellations. To make sure we didn't find each other, he bound each half's consciousness to what would eventually evolve into a human form and left us to wander the Earth in an endless search."

Alison and Lilian's expressions hadn't changed. They appeared unable to compute the information they'd just received. Porri couldn't say she was surprised, it was the reaction she'd been expecting. Standing up, she returned to the kitchen, leaving them time to process. It took about three minutes. "Ok, wait, you're saying you're actually a star?" Alison said, pointing up to the sky. "A star," she emphasized slowly. "You do understand that's …"

"Insane?" Sadal interjected from the doorway. He was sweating. Muscles bulging under his armor as he trod across the room toward Porri. His armor evaporating as he walked, leaving only the same sweats he had on before.

"I was going to say bat shit crazy," said Alison, a little less confidently. "But we'll take the PG version, sure. How are we supposed to believe this?"

"Look," Sadal said, "try to think in multi-dimensional terms. *We* exist on many different planes, simultaneously. Both as a star and as a human. Our bodies are mortal. They live and die just like yours. Our souls, on the other hand, our memories…. they are continuously reborn. Zeus wanted to make sure we lived in anguish."

"Anguish. Because you're separated," guessed Lilian.

"Exactly." Porri nodded. "Even if, by some miracle, we should find each other, Zeus will sense it as soon as we touch or spend too long in the other's presence."

Alison sat wide eyed. "So then what happens?"

Porri's eyes met Sadal's. "One of us dies," he said. "Only to be reborn as far away as possible."

Lilian looked back and forth between them. There was no doubt in her mind that they were telling the truth, but she was struggling. "This is... I can't wrap my brain around this. I know you're telling the truth, but I can't get myself to believe it."

Sadal, who's focus hadn't left Porri offered assistance. "Allow me to show you." He approached Porri, facing her. They held their hands up and placed their palms together. Suddenly the room burst to life with beams of light, nearly knocking Lilian and Alison off their bench. When Sadal and Porri released their grasp, the light faded and the room, which had seemed bright before, looked almost dark. "Do you understand now?" Sadal continued. "Porri and I are one. Together we are whole. The love that exists between us, there aren't words to describe in any language that humans have invented. To be separated from one another is the worst kind of torture."

Alison took Lilian's hand under the table. It was evident the two of them were on the verge of being completely overwhelmed and were fumbling to ground themselves. "Alright." Alison said slowly. "Okay. So, if all of this is true, why are you together now? I mean you just touched, why didn't someone die?"

"Nyx," Lilian replied, squeezing Alison's hand. "It has something to do with her, doesn't it?"

Sadal nodded. "Zeus is terrified of her. He's chosen to hide. He won't fight her. Which means we have to." He gestured toward the group outside.

Lilian took a moment, placing her face in her palms. "And my dad?" she asked finally. "What does he have to do with this?" Both Porri and Sadal remained quiet. It was obvious neither one of them wanted to answer her. She could sense them searching their brains for a way out.

"Please don't stop being honest now. I heard them say his name."

Sadal took a deep breath. "Lilian, ... your father is one of us."

Of all the things she had heard today, that was the one thing that knocked the wind out of her. There was no way. "That's not...that's not even.... he's never.... " She was lost. The words weren't there. She had to gather herself for a second. "I've never seen him do anything like this!" she cried. "I've never heard him *talk* about anything like this." She stood up from the bench. "Are you... are you sure we're talking about the same person?"

"Yes," Sadal replied softly, trying to calm her.

"Why isn't he here with you then?" Lilian demanded. "Who is his other half?" Sadal and Porri were silent again, both looking at the ground. It didn't take long for Lilian to realize that she didn't actually need them to answer. She already knew. "Shera." She half whispered to herself. Then turned to them, "Shera is his other half." Sadal lifted his head in response. "Why didn't he tell me anything?"

Sadal took a seat at the table and Porri joined

him. He gestured for Lilian to sit, but she was in too much of a state. "Because he doesn't remember," he soothed. "We were given a choice. If one of us wants to be released from this ...existence... then all we have to do is ask. It's within the power of our other half to release us. We're still immortal, but we would carry no memories of our true selves, our previous lives, or the other part of our soul. Lilian, he hasn't told you because he doesn't know. He has no memory of us, of the beginning, not even of Shera. We call it the vow. Just over a century ago he asked her to take it."

"And she just did it?" Lilian seemed on the verge of tears.

"She released him because she loves him. She released him because he asked and she couldn't bear to see him suffer." Porri said.

Dismayed, Lilian tried to understand. "So why didn't she ask him to release her too?"

Porri shook her head, "Never. Shera would live through a million hells before she lets his memory go. It's all she has left."

Lilian sank back down to the bench, facing away from the table. Alison took her hand again.

"I don't know what to say." She whimpered. "How many others have taken.. the vow?"

"No one," Sadal replied, almost harshly. Noticing the horrified expression on Lilian's face he continued, "I won't pretend I wasn't angry with him when Shera told me. I still am. But before you judge your father, you have to understand something. Shera and Cas, ... they were the larger star, the center of our circle. They were the most powerful of all of us and it was they that truly held us together. Each of us would move mountains to be with each other, but those two... their love was more profound than you can imagine. I honestly believe they could pull the fabric of the universe apart. It was even harder for them than it is for us. He simply couldn't watch her die or lose her anymore."

Tears had welled up in Lilian's eyes. "I can't believe he left her. But it... it makes sense.... It makes so much sense .... He's never been happy. I see him looking out the window like he's waiting for someone... After he and Mom split, I tried to get him to see other women, he just wasn't interested. I asked him once if he thought he would ever fall in love again and he said he hadn't even been in love with Mom... that love was something he couldn't reach. He's just been so cynical about it. But she was right there. The whole time? She must have hated my mother... hated me..."

Porri reached over to touch Lilian's shoulder. "Lilian, Shera loves you. She has watched you grow up. You were the child she could never give him. She may be a stranger to you, but she's always been there to protect you."

Lilian looked at her. "He never...had a child before?"

"We can't," Brach jumped in. Lilian and Alison both jolted, not having seen him come in. Brach walked over to the island and scooped up a chicken leg, taking a bite and continuing with a full mouth. "I mean, if one touch kills you then..." He didn't need to finish. Lilian got the idea.

Porri smiled at Lilian. "It took him a couple lifetimes, but..."

A hint of a smile formed on Lilian's otherwise stricken face as she looked at Michael, "...special..."

Everyone looked up to see Shera standing

in the doorway, leaning against the frame. She was wearing different jeans and a faded, green t-shirt. Her hair was damp and her eyes were just a bit red. She made eye contact with Lilian. "You're the daughter of a star, Lil." Shera knew that nobody but Cas called her that, but at this point she didn't care. "You and Michael have a fire inside you that no one else on this planet can lay claim to except us." She and Lilian continued to look at each other. Shera thought there was something different, an understanding, maybe even affection, that hadn't been there before. Eventually, she raised her attention to the courtyard and whistled. The noises outside ceased and they each filed into the room, walking through swirls of evaporating armor. Once everyone was in, Shera continued, "This is going to happen sooner than we hoped. I don't think we've more than another couple days. And she's going to start by going after Cas again."

"Again?" Asked Maia, breathing heavily.

"Last night. I heard him... his heart.... I couldn't see her, but I know she was there."

"Is he ok?" Lilian asked panicking.

"He's fine," Shera said calmly.

"Your sure? It was *her*? Not a..." Sadal inched toward her.

"Without a doubt," Shera confirmed. "I trust these two gave you a run down on the demon." She nodded toward Lilian and Alison. "And I expect there will be plenty more soon. I'm sorry, I know that's not what anyone wanted to hear and I wish..." She paused to keep the lump from rising in her throat. "I wish you all had more time. I don't know exactly what happened to scare her off, but ... she's not going to stay away. And my best guess is that she knows that killing him at the very least weakens us. Might I suggest that you take the night."

The room filled with a sadness. Dorsum scowled slightly and pressed his forehead to Mina's. Les took Maia's hand and pulled her close. She lay her head on his shoulder as they slowly left the room. Nunki reached up and ran her fingers through Sal's hair while he gently lifted her chin. They walked back outside followed by Brach and Resha, his arm around her shoulder and hers around his waist. Shera turned to Sadal and Porri. "I'm going back to the city. I've got to be close enough to protect him."

"What are you going to do, follow him around? He'll notice," protested Sadal.

"I'll figure something out," Shera assured him.

"Shera," Sadal began, "maybe you.... maybe you should tell him."

"No," Shera said abruptly.

"Shera...." Sadal started again.

"No," she shot again. "I will not break my promise to him."

"She'll kill you both, you realize that. And you know it won't be .... you'll be gone this time. There's no coming back from this," Sadal stared at her, visibly upset.

"What does that mean?" Lilian interjected.

Shera glanced at her. "We're a threat, Lilian. She'll erase us from existence. And it's a risk worth taking," she said back to Sadal. "I'll find a way to get close."

"He's going to a charity function tomorrow night. I can get you in. If we leave now, we'll make it in time." Lilian surprised everyone.

How is she not catatonic right now? Shera wondered. "You need to stay here."

"Michael and Alison will stay here. I'm going," Lilian said matter of factly.

It was clear she was not going to argue the point further, but Shera had to try. "Lilian..."

"That's *my* Dad," Lilian stated. "And I'm safer with you than anywhere else." Without wasting a beat she was standing up and going for her purse.

Shera was taken aback, almost touched. Six hours ago she'd been certain that this girl would never trust her, let alone be willing to help her. And she'd definitely given up on any idea of a bond. Now, she was willing to not only put her life in Shera's hands, but Cas's as well. Her heart fluttered a bit. Glad the air between them had finally been cleared, glad that Lilian knew the truth. While Alison pleaded with Lilian to be careful, she walked close to Sadal and Porri "Tomorrow..." she started to say.

"We'll be ready," Sadal replied without letting her finish.

Shera placed her hands on their shoulders and pulled them in, the three of them touching foreheads. Then she turned to Lilian who was standing next to Alison. She had Michael in her arms. Lilian contorted her mouth as though thinking about something then walked over and stopped in front of Shera with him. Meeting her eyes, Shera understood that she was giving her permission to be part of his life, however briefly it may be. Feeling tears start to swell up in her eyes again, Shera touched his little foot. He gazed up at her with an innocent and curious smile that both melted and broke her heart. She felt a renewed energy surge through her. She would tear Nyx limb-from-limb before letting harm come to this little soul. Forcing herself to look at the ground, Shera squeezed Lilian's arm. She understood. Shera couldn't afford to break down again. "I'll meet you in the car." Walking swiftly toward the front door, she snatched her backpack off the ground and swung it over her shoulder. *This is it*, she thought as she went, her dream and her nightmare all wrapped up into one.

CHAPTER 26

Shera tossed the keys onto the kitchen island. "Make yourself at home."

Lilian stepped cautiously into the apartment, not quite knowing what to expect. It was pretty extraordinary, actually. An open loft with high ceilings and brick walls. The kitchen on the right faced the living area that was dressed with a brown sofa that looked like something you could just sink into and fade away. There was a white coffee table littered with magazines, newspapers and books. See through bookshelves, piled with more books, separated the living and dining areas, and large windows let in sunlight that reflected off the white kitchen cabinets. To the right of the living area, on a platform four steps high, was the bedroom enclosed by three walls. Everything was Earth-toned and simple; messy yet clean. There wasn't a single piece of décor or furnishing that did not serve the purpose of either comfort or usefulness.

"Wow," Lilian mused. "This is kind of great. I wasn't sure if your tastes ran more like Dad's. Everything is so dark at his house."

"He wasn't always like that," Shera replied. "Used to be, he couldn't get enough of the light." She walked to the pantry. "Coffee?"

Lilian was browsing through the books. "Please, thank you. You have a lot of books."

"Believe it or not, this is nothing compared to Sadal's place. I like to read," Shera shrugged.

"I can see that. Have you read all of these?" Lilian asked doubtfully.

"Most of them, yes," chuckled Shera. "Keeps one from going insane." Lilian grunted which made Shera's brow furrow. "What?"

"Its just..." began Lilian. "I see a lot of history and politics here. I would think that having lived as long as you have, through the things you've lived through..... being interested in ... you know... mortal politics."

Shera smiled as she scooped coffee into the filter. "Yes, I can see how you might think that. But, in truth, having lived so many lives is exactly *why* I take such an interest. The fact that I've experienced existence through countless eyes. I can still feel the rib crushing corset I wore to court, I can see the breathtaking sunrises over the rice fields, I can smell the horrible combination of vomit and shit that I walked through on the streets." Shera finished pouring water into the coffee pot, flicked it on and turned toward Lilian. "I've been an heiress, a ward and a slave. Having seen the evils of dictatorship and felt the foot of tyranny on my throat, I can tell you that what exists now, this democracy, is as beautiful as it fragile. If you don't pay attention to it, don't protect and nurture it, what is fragile shatters. And freedom as you know it becomes nothing but a memory. Freedom is never more than one generation away from extinction."

"Ronald Reagan," Lilian said with a hint of a smile. "One of Dad's favorite quotes."

"Of course it is," Shera pulled open the cabinets and brought down two coffee mugs. She was glad of Lilian's company at the moment. Though, they hadn't chatted much up to this point. The majority of the ride back to the city was in silence. It was pretty clear Lilian was trying to process everything that had been thrown at her over the course of the previous 20 hours, but she seemed to have recovered slightly. She was still looking around Shera's living room when she spotted a book about antiques.

"Oh my God," she whispered to herself. "You have Dad's book."

"I do." Shera was putting a tray together with creamer and sugar.

"Did you know they interviewed him for part of this?" Lilian asked, sitting down on the sofa and opening it in her lap.

"I didn't at the time I bought it, no," Shera admitted. "It found me in a bookstore and I knew I needed to buy it. Didn't realize until I read through it why the urge had been so strong. He did well, not that I'm surprised."

"He tried to act like it wasn't a big deal, but I knew he was kind of puffed up about it," Lilian joked. "He even made it his coffee table book."

Shera laughed. She poured the coffee and brought the tray to where Lilian was sitting. Grabbing her own mug and taking a place on the other portion of the L-shaped sofa, she leaned back and took a sip while Lilian fixed her mug. Shera sighed, the coffee was warm and instantly calming. She closed her eyes and breathed in the aroma then held the mug to her chest, taking in its heat. When she opened her eyes she saw that Lilian was smirking at her oddly. "Coffee is sort of a religious experience for me," Shera explained earning a nod of understanding.

"So," Lilian said leaning back with her mug as well, "what now?"

Shera though for a second. "Now we wait for the event. You can introduce me as your friend, but I'm going to need to keep my distance. I don't know what sort of effect being near me will have on him. Maybe none at all, but I can't risk him... remembering anything. Not that I think that's likely to happen. That is, he shouldn't." Realizing she had been talking to herself for the latter half of that answer, Shera stopped herself by taking another drink.

"Okay. So, I'm assuming you have something for us to wear?" Lilian winced, there was definitely a tone of doubt in her voice. And for good reason.

Shera's eyes went wide. She hadn't thought of that. "Shit," she blurted. "Honestly, I hadn't even thought of that. I really don't. It's formal? I really don't. Shit." Lilian had set her coffee on the table and had her face buried in her hands. At first Shera thought she might be upset, but then understood that she was laughing. "Why on Earth are you laughing?"

Lilian raised her head, "Because I saw you battle a demon less than twenty four hours ago and you weren't the least bit bothered by it, compared to the full blown panic that is covering your face right now." She stood up. "Come on."

Shera looked horrified. "Where are we going?"

"Dress shopping," Lilian said, holding out her hand in an offer to help Shera up.

"Now?" Shera groaned. Couldn't they just stay here, finish their coffee and go in sweats? Even thinking it to herself she sounded stupid. She took a deep breath and let it out. "Alright." Setting her coffee down, she stood with Lilian and they made their way out of the apartment.

CHAPTER 27

God, I don't feel like doing this. Cas took a deep breath in and blew it out. He leaned against his sink, arms crossed, and eyed the tux jacket in front of him. He could feel his brain searching for an excuse or some emergency to invent, anything to get him out of his obligation to go to this damn event. But there was nothing. His company was one of the biggest donors and he had committed to attending. He hadn't been looking forward to it before, but the prospect of seeing Andrea and Meathead there made it worse. Accepting his fate, he reached for the jacket and slid it on then turned to the mirror so he could adjust it. The bathroom, much like the rest of his house, was dark and colorless. Gray, marble, double sinks beneath one large, unadorned mirror. Behind him, the wall was gray with black trim matching the black tile floor. He remembered the first time Lilian had set foot in this bathroom. She took one look and asked him if he was allergic to color. The thought made him smile. He wasn't, of course, he just had a distaste for it. It always felt that bright lights and a multitude of colors had the opposite effect as intended with most people. Instead of filling him with joy, he was weighed down with a sadness he couldn't quite explain. It's not that he enjoyed the dark so much as it kept him numb.

Straightening his cufflinks, he muttered to himself, "It's for a good cause.... It's for a good cause..." And it was, Cas liked this particular charity, ensuring basic needs for underprivileged kids, such as free lunches and home computers. He'd been fortunate in his upbringing. Despite being from a wealthy family, he'd never been handed anything. He had to work for every scrap he got, but it was always made clear to him that he had opportunities others didn't. He was taught discipline, then he was given the chance to put that discipline to use. He started his antique business when he was just out of college. Then he'd put in countless hours building up his clientele, first selling antiques, then seeking out specific pieces for high paying elites eager to impress, finally helping companies on a global scale invest in, excavate, price and sell their own. He was known the world over for having impeccable taste and a flawless record. If he said something was real, it was. Nobody questioned it. Cas had no idea what made him so good or passionate about this field, but he had a sixth sense about the authenticity of historical artifacts and he made it work to his advantage.

The least he could do is help ensure that children had the same opportunities he had. If it produced even one genius who helped change the world, it was worth the cost. He simply wished his donations didn't illicit invitations to things like this. Much as he was accustomed to wealth, he found it difficult to be around people of the same financial stature. A mix of snobs who donated for a badge of honor and looked down their noses at people whilst writing their checks, attention seekers, people who were defined solely by their fortunes and plenty of half naked women (plus more than a few men) looking for their future husbands. That last was the worst. By the end of the night there was, inevitably, some cleavage heavy blonde glued to his side, laughing way too hard at his jokes and struggling to keep up with any serious conversations that didn't involve the Kardashians.

They reminded him of all the reasons he'd married Andrea and it made him nauseous. There were good people there, of course, but they always managed to be overshadowed by the ones he couldn't stand.

He fiddled with his bowtie, stretched his neck from side to side and rolled his shoulders as though he was getting ready to step into the ring for a fight. "Okay, Ali." He said aloud to his reflection. Then thought of his next words..... *Let's do this?.... Let's get it on?....* he couldn't. Even just saying it to himself he would feel like an idiot. He thought for a second then settled on, "let's get drunk." He turned and flicked the light off as he strolled out of the room.

CHAPTER 28

Sitting in the back of the limousine, both Shera and Lilian were now dressed and nervous. It had felt pretty silly to them, dress shopping right before the apocalypse, but they hadn't much of a choice. Shera walked in and just grabbed the first thing on the rack that was her size, but Lilian had quickly seized her hand and put it back. "If we're going to do this, we may as well do it right," she had said.

"This is not really my thing," Shera replied uncomfortably. An unfortunate side effect of knowing your soulmate is a lack of interest in dating. Without any desire to impress the opposite sex throughout her lifetimes, Shera hadn't ever put much thought into her clothing. Focusing more on comfort, her current wardrobe consisted of mainly jeans, t-shirts, sweats, hoodies and a couple of jackets. She knew absolutely nothing about fashion and couldn't tell you the difference between Gucci and Coach if she had a gun to her head.

"Then allow me," Lilian offered. She browsed

through the store and selected three dresses for Shera to try on and two for herself.

Shera, naturally, picked the most comfortable of the three and hoped the process was over before Lilian dragged her over to the shoes. This was almost torture, she thought, way out of her zone. "Maybe I should just wear my armor," She joked.

Lilian chuckled a little bit while she found the right shoes for Shera's dress. "I thought the idea was not to stick out." She smiled at Shera as she handed her a pair to try on, catching her off guard.

"Thank you," Shera said quietly, taking the shoes, "And thank you for ...this."

"You're welcome," Lilian said affectionately.

Now, in the limousine, neither one of them really knew what to say. Or maybe they just both had too much to say and didn't know where to start. Eventually Lilian broke the silence. "He's not happy, you know," Shera had not been expecting that. She turned her head a bit in Lilian's direction, but didn't make eye contact. "He's never been happy. I think...even though he didn't know it...he's ...missed you."

"As much as I want to believe that, Lil...it shouldn't be possible," Shera said. "And all I've ever wanted was for him to find happiness, peace."

"I'm sorry...that he left you," Lilian said sincerely. "I'm just...sorry."

"Please don't let yourself wear guilt for him. It is what it is," Shera replied. "Don't be sorry. Besides, if he hadn't, you wouldn't be here."

"Do you forgive him?" Lilian asked.

"Yes," Shera whispered back.

"Do you still love him?" Lilian stared at her, sounding almost hopeful.

Shera took a moment. "Love..." she said, looking as though she was pondering the word.

Lilian took a guess, "Too strong a word?"

"Not strong enough," Shera explained. "It's too common. Too relatable. Cas is... every missing beat of my heart. He's what makes air breathable. What makes a melody music instead of just ...noise. I have spent thousands and thousands of years utterly consumed by him. Imagine the whole of the cosmos into a single person. That's what he is to me, what he will always be to me. My eternity."

Lilian was quiet for a few minutes, then she looked a Shera with tears welling up in her eyes. "I wish he hadn't....... I really wish he knew you."

The look on her face was almost too much for Shera. She reached out and lifted Lilian's chin. "I'm always with him, Lil. Even if he doesn't feel me anymore." Dropping her hand down, she took Lilian's. "You know, I must have imagined speaking to you a million times. I don't know that I believed I ever really would, but I never would have thought ...or wished it to be for this reason. I know that your world has been turned upside down and that I'm a part of that. I'm just...sorry... that we couldn't have met under better circumstances." Shera closed her eyes to get control of her emotions before continuing. "Just...please know that... watching you grow up... I am constantly astonished by the woman you have become. And I know ...I *know* your father is too."

Lilian didn't reply, she couldn't. But she squeezed Shera's hand hard and wiped away the tears from her face. Their hands remained tightly clasped as they both looked out their opposite windows. *It didn't seem fair*, Shera thought. To only now be able to tell her how much she meant... now, at the end. Turning down the final street, Shera could feel Cas getting closer and her heart began to race. *What am I going to say?* How could she meet his eyes without him seeing through her? *How the hell am I going to do this?*

CHAPTER 29

A small crowd gathered outside the gala event building. Red carpet had been laid out and an enormous red velvet banner hung over the entrance reading "For Under For All" followed by the logo of a two hearts stacked on their sides, the bottom one looking like a reflection in water. A few members of the press were snapping pictures of arriving patrons, yelling questions and jotting down names. People who had just arrived paused outside to greet others who hadn't yet made their way in. Cas stood among them, shaking hands and exchanging pleasantries with a fellow businessman whom he despised and his borderline inappropriately young date.

"I heard you had trouble with a Chinese investor the other day," the man said to Cas.

"No," Cas corrected, "no trouble at all. He had doubts and I laid them to rest."

"You know a friend of mine put in a bid for that job," the man teased, his date eyeing Cas like a sirloin in a steakhouse.

"Well, I'm sorry to disappoint." Cas mustered

his best fuck you smile. He was already getting annoyed. "Better luck next time." He started looking around for someone else that might get him out of this conversation. *Dammit, nobody.* Looked like he was going to have to start being rude. He'd hoped to put that off at least a half hour, or maybe until he'd made it into the building.

A limo pulled up to the curb, catching his eye. Dare he hope for someone he might want to talk to? An attendant rushed to open the door and a woman stepped out. Cas' heart stopped. She was …. exquisite. Small, toned and slightly pale, she wore a backless, floor length gown of sage green silk that draped off her shoulders. Her long, dark brown hair was pulled up, leaving whisps to frame her oval face. Cas stared, almost frozen in place, unable to tear his gaze away. The sound around him became distant and his vision tunneled. Then, the woman froze as well, an expression close to fear setting in before she turned her head directly toward him, her eyes finding his, as if she had sensed him there. Heat flushed his body. It seemed as though everyone around them melted away along with time itself.

The urge to rush to her was a force he'd never felt before. Cas had no idea how long they'd been standing there. Seconds, hours, days, but it wasn't until a flash of turquoise chiffon came into view and the woman in green, dazed and broke eye contact that he realized he hadn't been breathing. She was focused on the woman in turquoise, who was talking to her. Forcing himself to do the same he recognized the other woman and was instantly confused. *Lilian?*

Shera reminded herself to breathe. She hadn't been ready for that, not right away. *Calm down*, she thought. *Calm the fuck down.* Lilian appeared almost concerned at Shera's sudden lack of composure, but understood as soon as she saw Cas fixated on them. "Are you.." she started to ask, but Shera cut her off.

"I'm okay." She said. "Let's go." Shera felt herself flush as they made their way closer to Cas. She knew her hands were shaking. *This is ridiculous*, she scolded herself, *get it together. This is not the first time you've seen him.* Struggling to control her breathing she tried to concentrate on her task. *You're here to keep him safe. Them safe. To look for danger. That's it.* Cas was now no more than five feet away. *Shit. Just... don't look at him. Don't look at him.*

"Lil," she heard Cas say, "what are you doing here?"

Shera tried to observe the other people around them while Lilian answered. *Don't look, don't look, don't look,* she continued to chant to herself.

"Dad," Lilian beamed with her best forced smile, while also trying not to look relieved to see him. "Surprise. My friend here had an extra ticket and asked if I'd like to come." She gestured to Shera.

Don't look at him. Shera almost shouted to herself, knowing that Cas was staring at her. *Shit.* She looked at him. His scent drifted over to her and her heart felt as though it would burst into flames. There was no way he couldn't see right through her.

"Hello," Cas said to Shera. Her eyes, now fixed on his, were endless, as though there was another world within them. Her face was expressionless, almost statuesque, but her eyes conveyed such a mixture and intensity of emotion that he was nearly rendered speechless.

"Hello," she said back, softly.

Cas hesitated. Her voice. There was a familiarity to it. Had he...? "Do I know you?" he asked before he could stop himself.

"No," Shera replied quickly. *Yes.* She thought. *Better than anyone.*

"You seem very..." he continued.

"You don't know me," Shera interrupted. She couldn't allow him to entertain the idea.

Dammit, Cas chided himself, *you're freaking her out. Stop staring at her. Be normal. What the hell is wrong with you?* "My apologies." He placed one hand on his heart. "You have a familiar face...." *Stop staring.* "Allow me to introduce myself, I'm Cas Aion." He held out his hand to her, not realizing until that moment how much he wanted her to take it, how much he wanted to touch her skin.

Shera looked down at Cas' hand. She yearned to grasp it and never let go. To fall into him and let the world fade away. *You can't touch him.* She told herself. Those same, old words she had told herself, lifetime after lifetime. Just for a different reason now. Shera couldn't say for sure if not allowing herself to touch him was for his protection or for hers, but she knew it was necessary if she was going to get through the night. "I'm sorry," she said, finally, still looking at his outstretched palm and wracking her brain for an excuse. The first thing that came to mind sounded stupid, but she blurted it out. "Phobia." Unwilling to meet his gaze again, she brushed past him. "Lil, I'll be inside." *Please let there be a bar.* Clenching her hands she walked quickly through the doors.

Cas watched her intently, the motion of her body not lost on him. Turning his thoughts back, what had she just said? *Lil?* He thought he was the only one who called her Lil. Holding out his arm for his daughter, Lilian took it and they walked slowly toward the entrance.

"Did I say something wrong?" he asked her, nodding after her friend.

"No," Lilian insisted. "She has a... thing with touch."

"Ahh. Well, I'm glad you're here," he patted her hand. "Maybe this won't be such a drag after all."

"Careful what you wish for," Lilian muttered, encouraging a scowl from Cas.

He wasn't sure what that meant, but he was a bit preoccupied to care either. *Why did she seem so familiar? Where have I met her before?* He needed to probe Lilian for information. "So," he began, trying to seem casual, "where did you meet her?"

Lilian paused and raised her eyebrows. "In my backyard, actually....it was a ...party."

"Good, good.....and is she single?" Cas knew he was doing a poor job at seeming disinterested.

"No, Dad," Lilian stopped and faced him, "You can't....." she looked like she was searching for words.

"Lil, you've been trying to set me up with someone for years. Are you actually steering me away now?" Cas asked a little too desperately. Although he truly didn't understand. She *had* been nagging him to date since she was a little girl. You'd think she'd be thrilled that he showed curiosity.

"Listen to me," Lilian asserted. Taking Cas aback for a second. Was there a note of fear in her voice or was he imagining that? "She's just... been through a lot. Okay?... Please...just be careful with her." It didn't sound like a warning as much as a plea. He knew his daughter well enough to know when something was off and something was off. At the time he'd been distracted by a green dress and hazel eyes, but even then when Lilian first said hello he sensed a note in her greeting that wasn't quite right. Now she was looking up at him with an expression he'd never seen on her before. He couldn't place it, but it made him feel like a stranger to her.

"Alright," Cas relented, concerned. "Sweetheart, is something wrong?"

"Of course not," Lilian replied with a smile he knew to be insincere. "Why?"

"Because you seem distraught," he said. He'd never been dishonest with her before and wasn't about to start now. "And you're looking at me like... I don't know... you've got a strange look on your face."

Lilian took his arm again and started them moving the rest of the way toward the entrance. "I'm fine. And there's no look."

"Oh, there's a look," Cas assured.

"There's no look," Lilian repeated as they merged into the crowd making their way inside.

CHAPTER 30

Sadal and Brach stood on Lilian's back porch observing the backyard. Behind them, Maia's head appeared as she poked it through the door from inside. "Anything?" she asked.

"Not a thing," Brach called back.

"Well, you didn't expect any of it to be left, did you?" Sadal walked down the steps and onto the grass. "Alison said it burned up." He bent over and picked up the bat that Alison had dropped. Looking it over before tossing it back toward the porch he walked further out onto the grass toward a giant blackened patch. Kneeling down, he touched it. There was nothing there, no residue, just grass darkened by heat. Still, he felt sick to his stomach.

Brach approached behind him. "The scene of the crime," he half joked. "So what do you think?"

"At the moment?" Sadal stood, observing the size of the burned patch. "That we have our work cut out for us."

"Food is here!" Resha shouted from the door.

Brach looked back and gave a wave. "Be

honest with me, Sadal. You think we're going to die today?"

Sadal didn't reply immediately, appearing lost in thought. Eventually he looked directly at Brach and gripped the side of his arm assuringly. "No, my friend, I don't." Dropping his arm, the two of them walked back toward the house. "What's for dinner?"

"Cheeseburgers," Brach said excitedly.

Sadal shook his head an laughed. "Oh we are definitely not going to die today. I'm not having a cheeseburger as my last meal."

"What's wrong with cheeseburgers?" Brach sounded offended.

They stepped inside and shut the door behind them.

CHAPTER 31

You shouldn't be drinking, Shera chided herself then pushed the thought away as she took another sip of wine. *Screw it.* She needed to calm herself down. Being that close to and conversing with Cas had nearly sent her off the deep end. If possible, she missed him even more now and her heart was heavy with the weight of longing. He was so, so close. And what's worse, he seemed interested, which set a hope floating in front of her face like a fragile soap bubble even while knowing she'd have to crush it. Yes, things were different at the moment. Yes, she could touch him, kiss him without suffering the misery of losing him immediately. But who's to say that would last? If ... IF they were lucky enough to win, save the world and send Nyx spiraling back out to space... who's to say that Zeus wouldn't just reimpose the same rules. Bestow the same curse. Then she would have broken her word and betrayed his trust, for nothing. She didn't have a choice, she had to keep her distance. She wondered if she really had the strength to do this. Thankfully, there was an open bar. She leaned forward against it and placed her elbows on the counter, pressing her temple against her left fingertips. Heat traveled up her spine, making her shiver. She could feel his attention on her again.

About a hundred feet from her, Cas was engaged in distracted conversation with a museum director, a cellist and their wives. To be honest, Cas wasn't speaking nor listening much. Lilian had gone off to find her mother leaving him free to turn his thoughts toward ...her. She leaned against the bar, facing away from him. His gaze wandered from her shoulders down her bare back to the perfect curve of her hips. Why did she stand alone? What was the sadness he detected in her eyes? What was it about her that called to him so strongly? At last reaching his breaking point, he decided that he needed to go to her, to talk to her, to look into her again. Lifting his own wine to his lips, he swallowed the half glass that remained then excused himself from the couples and strode quickly toward the bar. He stopped just before he reached it, not more than a foot from her. His hand shook as he resisted the desire to reach out and run his fingertips across her back. He wasn't there for more than a split second before her head raised. Was it just him or were there goosebumps forming on her arms?

"Glass or conversation?" she asked, not looking at him.

"Excuse me?" Cas replied, taking the final step to her side.

"I was just wondering which ran dry first." She only regarded him for a moment, then became engrossed in her own drink. "But I see it was your glass."

Cas smirked. "It was both, actually. May I ask what you're drinking?"

"The pinot," she returned, still not looking at him.

"Of course you are," he said, managing to get a scowl and quick glance out of her.

"May I get you a refill?" The bartender appearing in front of them asked, "What are you drinking?"

"The pinot." Cas pushed his glass toward the bartender who filled it. "Thank you." Allowing himself a sideways peek at Shera. She was still staring intensely at her wine. Though she didn't seem to be looking at it as much as she was looking *away* from *him*. "I figured it out, by the way....."

"What is that?" she questioned.

"Where I know you from," he said calmly. Suddenly she turned her head toward him and he was paralyzed. Her face, not extraordinary, was still the most beautiful thing he'd ever seen, but it was her eyes that struck him dumb. The expression he saw there, like she was reaching out from within while holding back an ocean of something else. He lost track of time again. There was nothing and no one but the woman in front of him and he wanted to dive into her, shield her, protect her, consume her.

Shera was sure he must hear her heart pounding. The room around them turned into a blur of noise and passing shadows. There was only Cas in front of her. Nobody else existed. Her everything. Fear and hope had a stranglehold on her. He couldn't remember. It wasn't possible. He stared back at her with a familiar heat in his eyes. She had seen that same look in the many faces that he had worn over the ages and knew exactly what it meant. And exactly what the consequences were. She was on the verge of breaking. Forcing herself to speak, she tried to keep her body from trembling. "Well?" she said at last.

"Well what?" Cas asked, as if coming out of a trance.

Shera took a breath. "Where do you know me from?"

"Ah.." Cas shook his head, trying to resituate himself. "Um...the park. I saw you at the park."

Shera looked away again and exhaled, then half smiled. "You're right. Of course. You must have seen me at the park."

Cas was dazed and overcome with confusion. She seemed disappointed, yet relieved. He wanted her to look back at him. He wanted to know what she was thinking. He wanted her to keep talking. "Do your kids play there?" he reached.

"I can't have children," Shera spat, catching Cas off guard. He didn't quite know how to respond. Nor did he understand why her admission cut him so deeply.

"Oh...I'm... I'm sorry." Cas was searching for what to say. "I didn't mean to.."

"It's peaceful to me," Shera interrupted him, feeling guilty for having made him uncomfortable. "I like... hearing them play... laugh."

"Me too," he offered, gaining another glimpse of her eyes as she faced him. Another round of distorted time was about to hit him when Lilian appeared.

"Dad! There you are," she exclaimed, grabbing his arm and shooting a concerned glance at Shera.

Shera was flooded with relief. This had become nearly unbearable. "Where have you been?" she asked Lilian.

"With my mom," replied Lilian apologetically. "She and Arthur are here and they want you to join them." She braced herself while looking at Cas. He winced and Shera had to bite her lip to keep from grinning.

"Alright," Cas responded at length. "But only if..." He stared bewildered at Shera. *I still don't know her name.* How is it possible that he would run away with her if she asked him, but he still didn't know her name? "I'm sorry... I never got your name."

"Britney!" yelled Lilian. "I'm so sorry, I thought I said, this is Britney."

It was Shera's turn to wince. *Britney? Really, Lil, that's the best you could do? I don't look like a Britney.*

"Huh. You don't look like a Britney," Cas said. And she didn't. The name felt wrong to him. That was stupid, what possible reason could she have to lie about her name? "Well, I think I can bear it if you agree to join us." Of course, what he had really wanted to say was *I'm not even remotely ready to leave your side, so I'll only go if you're next to me.*

Shera saw the hope on his face and relented. "Sure. Thank you." He grabbed both of their wine glasses and handed hers to her, their fingers coming dangerously close to touching. Straightening her back she smiled at Lilian. "Lead the way."

Lilian and Cas walked arm in arm across the room while Shera followed closely behind.

CHAPTER 32

As the sun set in Lilian's backyard, the world seemed at peace. Were it any other day, one would assume they were just having a get-together. Children could be heard playing next door and spurts of laughter came from the age old companions while they exchanged stories and thought of times long gone. Les was trying his best to teach Maia how to catch with the baseball mitt while Nunki cheered her on and Sal yelled out suggestions. Even Alison appeared a bit more at ease than her nearly catatonic state earlier. Sadal thought it best she remain with them instead of staying behind at the temple alone and they had to be close to the city.

The table was littered with paper plates, napkins, cups and uneaten food that Brach would pick at every once in a while, between debating points with Sadal. They had moved on to films and were currently engrossed in an argument about the effects of the Star Wars franchise on the world in comparison to Homer in his time. Porri and Resha amused themselves by making fun of the men. Dorsum and Mina sat with them, but were engaged in conversation with Alison about her work in geopolitics. Michael sat contently on Porri's lap, getting more than enough attention since the group was taking turns fawning over him.

A cold gust of wind rushed overhead. Sadal stopped mid-sentence and threw his attention upwards. The sun was almost completely gone now and a sense of foreboding grew with the darkness. They could all feel it. Falling over them like a sudden rainstorm. There was a silent sort of exchange between all of them before they dropped what they were doing and started to clean up. It was almost time.

CHAPTER 33

Shera drew a deep breath. She never would have thought it possible, but she'd prefer battling demons right now. She sat at the table draped with a fancy, white tablecloth, black candles in gold holders, white and gold laced napkins and gold-plated silverware trying her best to be invisible. That was a hard task considering Andrea kept eying her with a combination of suspicion, competitiveness and curiosity. She sat across the circular table from Shera with Arthur and Arthur's secretary, a young, attractive redhead who was fixated on Cas. Lilian had tried to sit between Cas and Shera, but had been nudged out of the way at the last minute by Cas and pushed toward her mother. Shera wasn't sure if it's because he wanted to be closer to her or just further from his ex-wife. Either way, the move had quickly put her on Andrea's radar. She was quite certain that any minute now she'd be asked what she did for a living and pried for the reason that she was invited to such a prestigious event. Luckily, the topic at the table had turned to politics and she was spared an interrogation for the time being.

"No, no, no, no, no," Arthur argued. "I don't care what he said then. He's seen the error of his ways and everyone is bound to make a mistake. He's publicly come out against Turner. We can count on him. I'm sure of it."

"A mistake?" Cas blurted. "It wasn't a mistake, it was a u-turn. Not two months ago he was spewing completely different bullshit than yesterday. His goal is relevance not righteousness, he's playing to whatever direction the wind is blowing and whoever will keep him in that seat. How do you go from saying a man is unfit to hold any office, to saying nobody should hold this office *except* Turner, then completely dropping all support? He's a moral and ethical pretzel whose opinion mirrors the tide. He's done and he knows it. I'll bet he's already packed his office. 'Logic dictates that contradiction is the signal of defeat,'" Cas said slamming his fist on the table to make his point.

Shera could have sworn she caught a quick glance from him but dismissed it. What was he doing? Surely he wasn't trying to impress her.

Proof that his memory of her was completely gone or he would have known she thought he was being an ass. She was never a fan of showmanship. Maybe he was trying to impress Andrea or make her husband look like a fool. Whatever his intention, it was lost on her. The redhead on the other side of the table was eating it up, though. Nodding her approval at every word and trying to show as much of the ladies as possible. It wasn't that Shera wholly disagreed with his tangent, but there was always merit to making the unpopular choices in politics, to doing the right thing even if it costs you your seat. Politicians like that seemed few and far between now. But she had the distinct feeling that even he didn't completely buy in to what he was selling. Scowling slightly, she scanned the room again, reminding herself of what she was *actually* doing here.

"I apologize if we're boring you." Cas's voice brought her attention back to the table.

Looking over at him, she must have seemed puzzled then realized her expression had been misinterpreted when the redhead piped in. "It's okay, political discussions aren't for everyone," she said condescendingly to Shera.

Why this little shit, Shera thought. *Listen here, toddler...* Shera clenched her jaw and ignored the young woman, speaking directly to Cas. "You're mistaking imperviousness for boredom, I'm afraid. Your argument is flawed."

"Oh really?" Cas lit up, which confused her. He wasn't normally the kind of person to accept criticism. "Please.." He held out his hand, inviting her opinion.

Shera squinted her eyes slightly, expecting him to add a snide comment, but he didn't. "Look, I will grant you, the man filibustered his own bill, he's not exactly someone you should look at as the epitome of conviction. But... holding on to the notion that a person can't be driven to change their mind by anything, but a lust for power is just... it's a pretty cynical way to look at the world. Your mistake is comparing his previous path, which shouldn't factor into the equation at all. Perhaps you should simply judge him solely on his current one? 'In the evolution of real knowledge, contradiction marks the first step in progress toward victory.'" Cas's eyes were locked on her's. A hint of shame hidden in their depths. "It's the rest of your quote," Shera continued. "Which I expect you knew, and omitted, as it didn't support your argument. It's a mistake to assume the worst in people who may simply have a change of heart."

"Okay, I'm sorry," the redhead spoke up. "Are you saying that you liked Turner? You honestly don't believe he was the worst president?"

"Turner?" Shera stared at her incredulously. "I was strictly speaking about Mitchell, but if you're asking about my thoughts on Turner as a president, let me put it to you this way. When the office of the presidency was created his powers were very loosely defined, for one reason. All the members of the Continental Congress had already unanimously decided upon George Washington. Their idea of allowing him to form the powers of the president himself were based entirely on their opinion of his virtue and integrity. So if you ask yourself which of those virtuous characteristics Turner possesses, I hope the answer is none. The fact is, had it been Turner in Washington's place, they would have etched the powers of the office in stone prior to him taking the seat. No, I didn't care for him. No dictator can be looked at in a forgiving light and those who follow him blindly do so out of fear, hate or power lust." Back to Cas, "But those who question him, whatever their reasons, should be viewed behind the shades of a different lens."

Everyone was quiet for a moment, until Cas said to Shera, "It would seem you're trying to educate me ... or admonish me." He looked almost defensive, but not unmoved.

Shera lowered her head. Feeling ill for having embarrassed him, if she actually had. "Nothing like," she said softly. "Just conversing. "

"Conversing or debating?" Cas pushed. He had the distinct feeling that she had known he was trying to show off and she'd called him out on it. He was embarrassed, but not about how he appeared to anyone else at the table, just to her. The way that she had looked at him made him angry with himself.

"You know, there's another quote I read in an interview with a businessman I ... at one time... had the greatest admiration for," she said, seeming to sense his anger.

"And what is that?" Cas asked harshly,

expecting another one of his arguments to be spotlighted.

Shera met his eyes again, set cold by his tone. "There is a certain comfort in knowing you don't *have* to be the smartest one in the room." She didn't look away from him.

Cas was struck dumb. He felt like she had put a knife in his gut. This beautiful, intelligent, anomaly of a woman before him was tossing his emotions around like a wrestler in a ring. Minutes ago he'd been whirling in the air and now she'd slammed him to the ground, knocking the wind from his lungs.

"Who said that?" Lilian asked, seeming like she was in another dimension, but still next to him.

"I did," he answered her finally. He couldn't bring himself to leave Shera's eyes. He was lost in her. There was something lingering there that she wouldn't say. So much more.

"So, Brittney," Andrea began. "What do you do for a living?"

Cas watched Shera grimace suddenly, as if in pain and forcibly drop her gaze from his.

"Nothing of consequence. If you'll excuse

me, I'm out." She raised her wine glass to the table, got up and quickly walked away.

Much to the redhead's dismay, Cas hesitated for only a minute before excusing himself as well. He searched for the green dress through the sea of people and strode toward her so fast he was almost jogging. "Brittney!" he yelled. She didn't turn or even slow. "Brittney!" he shouted again, drawing some looks from the other guests. Still no reaction. Finally, he broke into a jog and cut her off. She stopped abruptly facing him.

"Hey. You didn't hear me calling you?" he asked.

"I didn't. Sorry," she replied, looking everywhere but at him.

"What is it with you?" he blurted out before he could stop himself. He couldn't help it. He wanted to be near her, to talk to her. The more she ignored him the more his frustration built. Especially since he got the sense that she was forcing herself to do it. "You've been dismissive toward me since the second we met. Did I say something to offend you?" He stood directly in front of her, close enough for her scent to run through his veins. She shot her eyes up at his and he felt his knees weaken slightly.

"Maybe I just don't enjoy being close to you," she suggested.

His body tensed. Her response stung, but somehow he knew she hadn't meant it. "Bullshit. What aren't you telling me?" He inched closer to her despite the tone of warning on her face. She wasn't more than a couple inches from him. He could feel the heat from her body on his. Her breath on his face as he towered over her. *Why do I feel this way?* Unable to restrain himself, he lifted his hand and grasped the side of her face, running his thumb along her cheekbone. The resistance in her eyes instantly melted away leaving a desperate plea mingled with longing in its place. Her head nuzzled into his hand, though she was trying to fight it.

"Please..." escaped from her lips, a single tear fell down her cheek and stopped at his thumb. Cas froze. She was begging him. He had never seen fear or passion so intense. In a rush of icy heat, his body flooded with an overwhelming and inexplicable need to protect this woman, this small, beautiful creature. It made no sense, on any level, but he knew in his core that he didn't want to exist in a world without her. Moving his hand around to the back of her head and neck, he started to bring her face toward his. The only thing in the universe he wanted in this moment was her. Her chest heaved as they drew closer, but there was no resistance. Her scent consumed him now and his head spun as their lips barely began to touch.

Suddenly the lights went out. Instantly coming back on, they then started to flicker violently. *What the hell?* Cas looked up at the lights slowly as if emerging from a stupor. There was a slight murmur of confusion in the room which escalated as the ground began to shake slightly. *Shit. Is it an earthquake?* He still held Shera's head in his hand. Looking down at her, he noticed both her eyes were shut tightly and her jaw had clenched.

"Dad!" Lilian yelled. He saw her running toward them. Shera's eyes opened revealing things he did not expect to see in that moment. Anger, acceptance, determination. She reached up, grasped Cas's hand, pulling it from her face just as Lilian reached them. Cas wanted to protest, but she turned toward Lilian and placed his hand in hers, then grabbed her shoulder.

Lilian looked terrified and on the verge of tears. *What the fuck is going on?* Cas thought. "You stay with him," Shera said to Lilian. "Promise me."

"I promise." Lilian was tearing up now and Shera put a hand under her chin.

"I love you, Lil," Shera said, "I always have." Cas was struck dumb again. *Why did she say that?* Why had she sounded so earnest? Why was Lilian so upset? Why the hell did he feel like the world was ending and he was the only one who didn't know what the fuck was happening? Shera paused and turned her body toward him like she was going to say something but didn't look at him.

He almost spoke, but stopped when a sound shattered the atmosphere of the room. A horrendous growl that shook the floor again. It was coming from outside. Without a word, Shera faced away from them and ran toward the entrance, toward the sound.

CHAPTER 34

Sergeant Jack Sorinson hadn't the faintest clue what he was in for. The Humvee was maxed out as it sped through the streets and he checked their location for the 50th time. The rest of the caravan was close behind them. Thankfully, the streets had been cleared in time. Flashing lights dotted their path, like breadcrumbs guiding them…. well, it wasn't guiding them fucking home, that's for sure. The local police had been able to push all civilian motor vehicles to a single lane, allowing them to plow ahead without hindrances, a task that would otherwise have been impossible during rush hour. He reached up and pulled at the straps of his helmet digging into his neck then shot a glance at corporal Tennyson behind the wheel. Tennyson was sitting straight up and chewing the inside of his lip nervously. Setting his jaw for an upcoming turn, he took it a little too tightly and clipped the curb.

"Shit," Tennyson gasped.

"Jesus, Tenny," Sorinson spat as the Humvee jolted to the side.

"My bad, Sergeant." Tennyson said apologetically, knowing better than to actually apologize. The last thing he wanted was a sorry sergeant retort right now.

Letting it slide, Sorinson checked the map again. He couldn't believe where they were going. Hell, he couldn't believe what they were doing. Every military unit in the country had been put on alert four days ago when the mist appeared. The pentagon made sure the media played it off as a non-threatening anomaly, but the fact is they had absolutely no idea what it was or where it was going once it had entered the atmosphere and dropped off their radar. Everyone had been put at REDCON-3 in case it showed up again. And it had. Here, in his city, less than an hour ago. Naturally, his National Guard unit was the closest. They'd been told to mount up a half hour later and given interception coordinates.

Sorinson picked up the radio, speaking as loudly and clearly as possible. "Motordog 2, this is Motordog 1, come in."

The radio crackled to life, static interference

slightly muffling the voice on the other end. "Motordog 1, Motordog 2. Go ahead."

"Motordog 2, Motordog 1. We are approaching intercept zone. Proceed to designated security point. Weapons hot. How copy?"

"Motordog 1, Motordog 2. Wilco. Out."

"Motordog 1 out." Sorinson finished, returning the handset to its cradle. He could feel Tennyson fidgeting next to him. "Calm your tits, Tenny. There may not even be anything there."

"Do you think they know what it is and just aren't telling us, Sergeant?" Tennyson asked.

"I have no idea," Sorinson said honestly. "Try not to think about it. Stay on task. Just drive, stop, and keep her running, Corporal. Too easy, right?"

"Too eee..." Tennyson started to repeat under his breath then trailed off.

Sorinson had been looking at the building ahead and to the left. There was a giant banner hanging from it and a red carpet had been rolled out to the entrance. He could barely see the shape of a woman appear there, a long, green dress billowing in the breeze. His attention would have remained on her had the Humvee not thrown him back against the seat. Tennyson was on the breaks hard, the tires squealed beneath them as the vehicle continued to slide forward and turn slightly to the left before halting. He could hear the trailing caravan start to break quickly as well, swerving to avoid hitting each other.

"Tennyson, what the fuck?" Yelled Sorinson, "This isn't..." he stopped. Tennyson was as white as a ghost and his eyes were wide with terror. He was looking at something just to the right of Sorinson's shoulder. Sorinson's stomach dropped as he slowly turned his head. There in the road behind him.... finding no other word for it... was a monster.

There wasn't time to exit the vehicle, there wasn't time to grab the radio, there wasn't even time to scream. It was on them in an instant. An enormous, skeletal hand stinking of burning flesh broke through the window of the Humvee and found his neck. Searing pain shot through him, as if his body was on fire. He felt himself get tugged through the window like a ragdoll, feet dangling in the air. Then, before him, a massive skeletal face, partially covered in what looked like charred meat. There were no eyes, just sockets. Sockets full of fire and rage. In spite of his body burning he could still feel the heat coming off this thing, it's acrid smell filling his lungs. He heard screaming and something else, gunfire? He couldn't breathe. He couldn't think. All he could see was this horrid face, and those terrible eyes. Then, nothing.

Sorinson was in darkness. There was no monster, there were no sounds, there was no heat. There was nothing. Starting to wonder if he was dead, he saw a tiny shape come into view. Margaret? His daughter. What was *she* doing here?

"Mar-pie?" he called out to her. But she didn't respond. She looked almost lost. Slowly around him the darkness faded, a black mist being lifted like a fog, to reveal his home. His kitchen. Margaret was in front of him, holding her favorite doll and his wife stood at the stove, stirring food in a hot pan.

"Honey!" Sorinson cried out, practically running to her. She didn't respond, or even look at him. "Honey?" He reached his hand out to touch her shoulder and it passed through her as though she were made of air. "Oh God." He quivered. "Oh God...... Mar-pie? Baby can you hear me?" He pleaded with his daughter, but she didn't acknowledge him. "No, no, no, no, no." He placed his hands over his eyes. Weeping. "Oh God, I'm dead."

"Mommy," Margaret called to her mother.

"Yes, Baby," his wife said, attention remaining at the stove.

"Can you start the movie over?" whined Margaret. Giving her mother virtually no time to reply, she whined again. "Mommy, please."

"Yes, Baby. I'll start the Minions over for you. Just give Mommy a second, okay?" his wife replied, turning the burner down slightly and continuing to stir.

Suddenly the back door slammed open, earning a shriek from Margaret and his wife swung around. Bewildered, Sorinson watched four men wearing masks enter his house. "Who the fuck are you?" he yelled instinctively, "Get the fuck out of my house!" His wife snatched Margaret up then grabed the hot pan off the stove and hurled it at the intruders. Dodging out of the way, they started laughing. Sorinson tried to place his body between his family and the advancing men, but it made no difference. Screaming for help, his wife started to make for the other room, but one of the men grabed her and pulled her backward. Prying Margaret from her hands and throwing her toward the table. Three of them surround her while the other made his way to the floor with his little girl. Sorinson was violently swinging at the men, but nothing he did made any difference. He could do nothing. His family. All he could do was watch in horror as the scene unfolded in front of him. Feeling his helplessness claw at him, he grabbed his hair as though trying to rip it out, no longer able to tell if the screams of agony were from his daughter, his wife or himself. Once the intruders had their fill, three of them left and the room fell silent, but for faint sobs. Sorinson's wife fell to the floor and crawled toward her daughter, cradling her. The single man who stayed behind walked to them, wielding a pistol, and only hesitated long enough to see the fear. Sorinson's last, horrible scream was drowned out by two gunshots reverberating throughout the house. Shaking, sick, face wet with tears and snot, Sorinson was once again plunged into darkness.

After a moment, a tiny shape appears. Margaret, holding her favorite doll. When the mist lifts to reveal their kitchen again, his wife at the stove. "Honey?" Sorinson's plea is barely audible.

"Mommy," Margaret called to her mother.

"Yes, Baby," his wife said, attention remaining at the stove.

"Can you start the movie over?" whined Margaret. Giving her mother virtually no time to reply she whined again, "Mommy, please."

"Oh God, no." Sorinson shakes his head. "No. This can't.... not again... "

"Yes, Baby. I'll start the Minions over for you. Just give Mommy a second, okay?" His wife replied, turning the burner down slightly and continuing to stir.

The door slams open and the four men enter. Sorinson unleashes all this fury to no avail as the horror show plays out again before the mist, again, descends.

Then, after a moment, a tiny shape appears.

CHAPTER 35

Shera stood for a moment in the building's entrance. Cool breeze catching her, carrying the scent of rotten flesh to her from across the street. It wasn't Nyx, but it *was* one of her demons, and she was willing to bet this one wasn't alone. Its attention had been turned to a slew of military vehicles that had stopped abruptly, nearly slamming into one another. *Fuck*, Shera thought. She started to move forward, but it had already broken through the window and grabbed one of the soldiers by the neck. Holding him up she saw some of the mist surrounding the creature seep into the soldier's mouth and nose. In the chaos that ensued, yelling and gunshots rang through the air. The first soldier had been released from the grip of the demon and dropped to the ground. He wasn't dead, but he wasn't here either. He looked confused, then began flying into an insane, desperate rage. The demon's focus now turned to the remaining soldiers.

"Hey," Shera said quietly, knowing it could hear her. It stopped and turned its body toward her. "They're not the ones you need to worry about," she continued, moving toward it.

Behind her, Cas and Lilian appeared, followed by others who had heard the sound of gunshots. They stood transfixed as Shera, walking away from them and toward the thing, morphed. Bursts of light covered her body as she strode forward. The green silk gown giving way, one section at a time, to gleaming armor with a sword and shield that seemed to have been made of a million diamonds, reflecting the moon and casting beams of starlight in every direction.

Risking a quick look behind her, Shera saw a crowd gathering, Cas and Lilian among them. *Dammit. They were supposed to stay inside.* She couldn't concentrate if... closing her eyes, she touched the emerald gem embedded in the chest of her armor. *Please let me find the strength. Please.* "Enkavma." Icy heat exploded from her core and ran down her right arm, kneeling down, she slammed her sword toward the Earth, light shooting from the tip and traveling back toward the gathering onlookers, spreading over the ground like water. Once it reached them, it broke from the surface and rose straight upward. A wall of transparent light had formed in front of the building and the crowd.

Cas, who had been paralyzed by the scene in front of him, jumped back as the wall skyrocketed right in front of his face. *What the fuck?* It looked like clear, glowing water, a hint of his reflection staring back. He reached out, it was solid. Like glass. *What the fuck?* The phrase kept repeating itself in his head. What he was seeing defied the laws of reality. It didn't make any sense. Lilian clutched his arm and he looked at her. She was watching intently, but there was something off. Her face didn't bear the same expression of sheer terror and disbelief as everyone else. She wasn't screaming, or faint, or rendered motionless by the impossible happening before them. It only took a second to realize what was missing, surprise. There, buried under the weight of worry and anxiety, was the betrayal of expectancy. She knew this was going to happen. "What is going on?" he demanded of her. She opened her mouth, like she was going to answer, but couldn't find the words. Instead, she looked away from him. He wasn't going to get an answer out of her. Not now. He stared back through the wall toward the woman. She was on her feet and sprinting toward the creature. That thing was something out of a horror film. A giant. Half melted and burning from the inside. It had to be standing at least nine feet tall with a wingspan twice as long. It was monstrous. She looked miniature by comparison. But there she was, running *towards* it. Fearless.

The demon bounded for Shera and, within a few strides, it met her. A blast of heat and rot hit Shera in the face. She squinted her eyes and clenched her jaw tight. It reached for her with both arms and she brought her shield across her body, knocking them together. In one movement she swung her sword upward, severing its arms at an angle below the elbows, then around to sever the right leg below the knee. It squealed in agony, spreading it's stumps out to its side, falling to one knee and opening its wings with a force that sent a gust of hot wind at her. Not hesitating, Shera jumped, using its in-tact leg to launch herself upward and burry her sword to the hilt under its chin, pushing up until the hilt was even with the nose then dragging it with her as she fell back to the ground, nearly cutting it in half. She stood in front of it, her sword still encased in its stomach, then placed her foot on its mid-section and kicked away hard, freeing her sword as it collapsed backward.

For a brief moment, nothing could be heard. No people, no gunshots, nothing. The calm before the storm. Then, a deafening howl, like a thousand people being burned alive, broke the stillness and echoed off the surrounding buildings. There couldn't have been a soul for 20 miles that didn't cover their ears and shrink to the ground. Except Shera. She kept her face locked on the black mist forming in the distance, watching it expand horizontally, certain that what she was hearing was Nyx speaking, and in a language that only she could understand.

"Lay down your sword, Sheratan." the voice conjuring images of countless hands clawing in desperation and darkness for escape. It changed continuously, akin to a child one second, a man the next, a grandmother the next, but always unnatural, always steeped in hatred.

Shera's eyes narrowed. "You know I won't."

"You can't save them," Nyx crowed then,

in a near whisper, "You're not strong enough alone."

Shera didn't respond.

"Give up!" Nyx shrieked again, loudly.

Shera glared into the spreading darkness ahead. "I don't have to tell you I'll die first."

"No, you won't," Nyx sang almost sweetly. Then, in a man's guttural voice, "but he will."

A sliver of a shadow flew past Shera and she spun her head to follow its path. It plowed into the light wall directly in front of Cas then bounced off and took the shape of another demon. Cas stood on the other side, bewildered. Shera's heart skipped a beat. She rushed toward the demon. It turned away from Cas in time to see her, just not in time to react. She had launched her shield in its direction, slicing through the neck like butter and lodging itself in the light wall. Just as the body fell and burst into ash and flame Shera reached the wall, ran up it, grabbed hold of her shield and pulled herself backward, flipping back and throwing the demon's head like a fireball toward Nyx. The resulting shriek from Nyx had everyone cowering again, hands covering their ears. Shera walked forward, pure hatred for Nyx running through her veins. Not him, she thought, and not *my* world. Out of the dark expanse before her, shapes began to emerge. Like a damn holding back another dimension, it burst, letting a flood of demons come forth.

Shera let out a sharp breath. "Now would be a good time, Guys," seeing no sign of them. Evidently she was going to have to do this on her own for a while. She put about 10 feet of distance between herself and the wall, she couldn't risk more than that, then braced herself for the onslaught. *Just don't let any of them pass,* she told herself. In the blink of an eye two of them were on her. Kneeling down she curved her sword toward the earth in front of her and stabbed the demon on her right in the leg then, withdrawing her sword and standing at the same time, she swung it upward, slicing at the ribs of the demon on her left. Whirling the sword over her head and flipping the hilt in her hand, she buried it in the pelvis of the demon on her right then turned herself back around hard while jumping to withdraw it and plunge it into the stomach of the other. The one on her right stumbled while the other gripped at its midsection. Together they tried to grab at her. She was able to elude one, but the demon on her left caught her sword arm, and a searing pain rippled through her body. Screaming out, Shera planted her feet and threw her shield up towards the demon's head, freeing herself as it sliced off its face and the upper portion of its skull. With another flash of light, her shield reappeared on her arm. The second demon lunged at her, trying to skewer her with its spear, but missing her as she ducked and driving it hard into the ground. Seizing the moment, Shera put her foot on the end of the spear and split it with her sword, leaving a sharp edge jutting up from the concrete. Then, throwing herself forward between the demon's legs, she severed it's remaining good leg, knocking it forward. The demon's head came down on the jagged spear edge and it squirmed before bursting into flames.

Cas was near insanity. He could do nothing but watch as she was out there alone. He beat repeatedly on the light wall, trying to get to her, but it was impenetrable. He'd probably be nothing but a burden out there. He had no idea how to fight and she could clearly handle herself, but he couldn't just stand here. There were too many of them. There was a dammed army coming out of that mist. Hearing her call out in pain when that thing grabbed her sent him into a frenzy. "God dammit!" He slammed his fists against the wall. *There had to be a way to get out of here.* Maybe he could go around it. "I've got to get out there." He turned to move pass Lilian, but she stopped him.

"Where are you going?" she said, grabbing at him.

"I have to get out there," he repeated.

"Daddy, you can't," she pleaded.

"I can't just watch! She's all alone out there." He was on the verge of losing it.

"No, you can't!" She held on to him with all her strength. "You can't go out there. She needs you to stay here."

"I have to do something!" he yelled, pushing back at her, then turning to find a way out.

"Daddy, if you go out there she'll die!" Lilian cried. Cas stopped then slowly turned back to her. "She'll die to save you."

Cas didn't know what to make of what she was saying. "You mean anyone."

Lilian had the look of a guilty child who had betrayed a secret. "No, Daddy. *You*. Please. Please. You can't go out there. She *needs* you to stay here."

Him? *Why the hell would this woman die for me?* He reached up and gripped his hair so tightly his head hurt, while he looked back through the wall. She had managed to kill the second one, but there were three more right behind her. Cas' body was overwhelmed with desperation to get to her, but the fear Lilian instilled by telling him he'd just be placing her life in more danger was keeping him rooted. He pressed his forehead against the wall, certain that any moment he would lose his mind, watching helplessly as the three demons closed in on her. She stood her ground and faced them head on. But wait, there was something...... Cas held his breath when he saw bright lights appear behind the creatures, moving back and forth like a wave. Before they knew what was happening, the demons were shredded from behind. Pieces of them flew in every direction, hitting the ground in piles of flaming flesh. It wasn't until he saw the group of people surrounded by light, wearing the same glittering armor, that he remembered to breathe. Relief flooded him. There were more. There were more of her. One, a large man, gripped the woman's shoulder and started speaking. Cas couldn't hear what they were saying, but she clapped her hand over the man's then gestured with her head back toward where Cas was standing. The man's eyes followed and he stared in Cas' direction. Cas was taken aback. *What the hell?* The man seemed familiar to him. Did he know this person? Why was he looking at him? Cas shifted uncomfortably, there was something close to anger in the man's expression and he felt suddenly flushed with shame that he didn't understand.

Shera had to swallow back her emotion when she saw the demons in front of her being ripped apart and her friends coming forward. "What, were you stuck in traffic?" she asked sarcastically, through a smile.

"We hit all the red lights." Sadal made his way to her side. "Every. Single. One." He placed his hand on her shoulder. "Are you ok?"

"I'm ok." Shera breathed heavily, reaching up and placing her hand over his. "Glad you're here."

"Cas?" Sadal sensed he was close by. Shera just nodded and gestured her head back toward the light wall. Sadal's eyes quickly scanned the crowd. She knew he had spotted Cas when she saw the anger. "He should be with us," he said, now focused back on her.

"We can't force him to remember, Sadal," she shook her head. "Are you ready?" she asked Brach and Resha, who had appeared. They, too, were looking back at Cas.

"He doesn't remember anything?" The hope in Resha's voice was hard to miss.

"He doesn't," Shera assured. "We're on our own."

"Great," Brach muttered.

Dorsum, Mina, Les, Maia and Porri joined them. All taking turns looking in Cas' direction. The advancing army had paused when the ten of them appeared. Undoubtedly, not knowing what they were capable of, Nyx was hesitant and ordered a halt. For now, the demons stood motionless before the mist. "Has she shown herself yet?" Dorsum questioned.

"No," Shera said, but she's there. Cowering.

They stood still. Nobody said anything, but they were all thinking the same thing. There was a very high chance that they could be facing their last moments. Countless lifetimes ending here, now. As they had begun, in a way. All of them whole. Almost all of them.

"Well," began Maia to Les, placing her hand on his chest, "if these are our last breaths, at least they'll be together." Les brought her forehead to his and they closed their eyes. The others followed suit. Shera watched, heartbroken as her family took their last seconds together. Nunki put her arms around Sal, Mina and Dorsum entwined their fingers and stared into each other's eyes, Brach held Resha from behind and buried his face into her neck while she rested her hand on his head, Sadal held his hand out to Porri and pulled her toward him, their faces nuzzled together in an almost kiss. Shera wanted to scream. A fresh loathing for Zeus swelled inside her. The cruelty of separating them was outdone only by this, allowing them to be together for the blink of an eye only to lose one another forever. Her body began to shake uncontrollably. She wanted revenge. For Cas. For these beings who she loved. For Lilian and Michael. For this world. Warm tears fell down her cheeks. Maia glanced at Shera, thinking she was upset about Cas. "Shera..." she started.

"I have *you*," Shera stopped her. "All of you." She glared defiantly at the mist. "And this is not your last breath." Slamming her sword against her shield the frequency punctured the air and echoed off every surface. The sound seemed to disturb the demons who leaned in toward her, snarling. Walking past her friends and closer to the army, she slammed the sword and shield together again. And again. And again. The high pitch starting to sound like a thunderous hammering. "Nyx!" she screamed. " Show your fucking face!"

Nyx bellowed, shaking the ground beneath them and her army began to move. Shera was unaffected. The power building inside her was bursting out, seeping through her fingertips. Driven by a combination of love for her companions, for Cas, and a hatred for all that had been done to them, she sprung forward, launched herself off the ground and turned herself in the air. Leaving her hands, her shield hurled toward the army, spinning, encased in the same material that made the light wall. It looked like an enormous circular saw, starting at one end of the demon army and moving straight down the line, cutting the first two rows of demons in half. A flash of diamond, light and flame. Then, in a beam of light, her shield reappeared on her arm. The raging moan from Nyx was echoed in her demons and they all prepared themselves to run at her.

Shera turned her head toward her friends. "Now."

Without hesitation, they each faced their half and placed their palms together. The transformation was instantaneous and awe-inspiring. The two bodies joined, emitting a prism of light and growing to a height twice that of the demons. Their eyes glowing an astonishing blue , each gripping a massive sword and shield. Five light warriors, Magnetars, now stood behind Shera, making her seem like a doll in comparison. For a very brief second, all was still. Then, with a roar from Nyx, the army of demons, sprinted toward them.

CHAPTER 36

Cas had lost all sense of reality. He couldn't begin to understand what he was looking at much less the fact that all of it seemed eerily familiar. The way each of them had stared at him, the sadness he felt when he saw them together, and now, a stirring in his core as the couples merged and transformed into massive beings of pure light. Ten of them had become five just in time for the army of creatures to charge. *She* hadn't changed, though. Why? Where was the person she was supposed to change with? He had to admit to himself that he was glad there hadn't been a man with her, the envy might have been unbearable. On the other hand, so was the guilt he felt for preferring her to be alone. She was completely vulnerable. "Why doesn't she change?" he asked, not really sure to whom the question was directed.

"She can't, Dad," Lilian responded.

Cas looked at Lilian. "Where is the man who is supposed to be with her?"

Lilian thought for a second. "He left her."

Clearly feeling like she might betray something further, she turned her head back to the battle.

Cas felt suddenly sick. *Who in their right mind would leave her?* The light warriors plowed into the oncoming wave of demons. They seemed almost unmatched. One swing of their sword dispatched dozens of demons into flying chunks of fiery flesh. The ones who made it past came upon the woman whose fury had doubled. Her body was almost indistinguishable from her sword and shield as she moved, killing demon after demon without tiring. Hope kindled in Cas that there might be an end, that these warriors and this woman would either kill every creature or drive them back into the shadow. But that hope slowly dissipated. They didn't stop, the demons. More and more came charging out of the blackness, there was no end. Out of nowhere, a black shape, like a cannon ball, came hurling toward them and struck the light wall, causing it to shake. Cas grabbed a hold of Lilian and made her duck with him just before impact. Looking back through the wall, he saw the woman run towards them, something close to panic on her face, and stop about five feet away before turning around to continue fighting. *Jesus, she is protecting us.* A second cannonball struck the wall. "Fuck!" he yelled, keeping Lilian in a crouching position. If possible, the woman was moving even faster, feet barely touching the ground as she slaughtered one demon after another when, just for a moment, she paused, chest heaving, to look back at Cas. He stood, placing a hand on the wall and stared at her. Their eyes locked and everything around them disappeared. Every cell inside of him wanted to go to her, to hold her, to shield her, to take her in his arms and never release her. He didn't see the other people. He didn't see the battle. He didn't see the demon behind her. But as the cry of pain left her lips when the spear sliced into her side, he let out a scream that should have shattered the wall.

Shera fell to her knees as her side was ripped open. The pain from her ribcage erased all thoughts of anything else from her brain. All the air had escaped from her lungs and she struggled to take a breath. She saw Cas on the other side of the wall, screaming. *Fight.* Shera told herself, *get up and fight.* Her thoughts reformed and she swung around, holding her shield tightly to her side. With agonizing effort she knocked the demon's spear skyward and put a deep gash into its chest. It hunched over, gripping its chest and she drove her sword into the side of its skull.

Trying to take shallow breaths, she faced the next two coming at her. Lunging backward, she threw both her sword and shield behind her where they ricocheted off the ground and flew back up over her, embedding themselves in the demon's heads. The move sent a torturous wave throughout her body and she tried to inhale. Her sight grew blurry while she labored to stay on her feet. She had to keep fighting. *Cas.* He was all she could think of. Closing her eyes, she allowed herself to see his face. Hear his voice. She allowed herself to do the one thing she'd been trying to push down for the last two centuries, love him. Love him completely. Love him with the fury of a nova that could shred the galaxy. Biting into her lip, she felt tears well up as she took a deep breath. She pushed herself to her feet and gripped the sword tightly, gritting her teeth. Bracing herself for the next three demons. Throwing her shield, it lodged itself in the midsection of the first demon. She sprang forward and jumped, using it to send her flying high enough to bring her sword down on the skull of the next demon. As she dropped to the ground, she tried to gather herself. The pain left her feeling on the verge of vomiting. Spinning around she had intended to go for the next demon's legs, but she wasn't moving quickly enough. It was already on top of her. It swung its arm, hitting her square in the chest and sending her flying backward. She hit the pavement hard, gasping for air and coughing up a bit of blood.

The sounds of the world suddenly seemed far away. The ground was cool. She wanted to lay there. Take a minute. She just needed a minute. Out of the corner of her eye, she could see the demon approaching. As if in slow motion. She needed to move. Trying to lift her sword, she realized she couldn't. Her body wasn't responding. *Dammit, Shera, get the fuck up!* Trying again, her limbs didn't budge. Nothing. This was it. This was it. She was going to die. She felt no fear, only sadness. She focused all her strength into turning her head. She needed to see his face. He was there, so close, she could almost touch him. The familiar stab of loss pierced her soul and overwhelmed her body. At least she could take comfort in knowing that seeing her die again wouldn't break him. Not this time. So many centuries of longing, needing to be with only him. And she never would. Her heart wept in her chest. *Please, please keep them safe*, she mentally begged her friends. Cas looked consumed by madness as their eyes met and the world fell away again. The only thing she could hear was the sound of her tears hitting the pavement. Then, though knowing he could never truly understand, she whispered to him. "I love you." The demon was over her, the sickening stench and heat cutting into her already shallow breaths. Slowly, she turned her face upward, taking in the monster with melted flesh and a double pointed spear raised above its head. It was time. She closed her eyes and waited.

In the distance she could make out someone calling her name, then another yelling, "Wake up! Help her!"

Cas was pounding his fists against the wall, frantically. "No, no, no, no, no! Get the fuck away from her!" The demon was getting closer, its wings spread to their full expanse, plumes of heat and flame trailing behind it. The helpless frenzy had taken over again and he was desperate for a way to get to her. She was right there. He had to get to her. "I'll fucking kill you!" he screamed at the demon. "Get away from her!" He couldn't do this, he couldn't watch her die. He stared at her motionless body on the ground. Her head turned toward him and their eyes met. They were filled with bottomless pain and sorrow. He would give anything in this moment to take her face in his hands, to eradicate her suffering. To plunge into the timelessness beneath her agony. This woman, *she* was what he had been waiting for, searching for. *She* was what called to him from the sky. It made no sense. But she was his reason for living, he knew it in his core. And he was about to lose her. Tears fell from her face as she looked over at him and he was struck dumb when he saw her lips form those three words. His heart fell to his gut. She had meant it. What's more, he *felt* it. He loved her, too, inexplicably, uncontrollably. As she closed her eyes another voice drifted to him, a voice he knew well. Lilian. She was still beside him, crying and slamming her palms against the wall. When she yelled something that sent his world into a full on spiral.

"Shera!"

A montage of images hit Cas like a truck, practically throwing him backwards. Stars, burning brighter than anything else in the sky. A feeling of wholeness, complete peace, power. Six moving as one. Then, separation and devastation. Endless searching. Traveling. Wandering and hoping. A slew of faces, women, all different, but all the same. Longing, loss and unimaginable grief. And love, always love, of a kind that can't possibly be described in any language of Man. The images came crashing to a halt on an oceanside cliff where he held the other half of his soul in his arms as she died. "Ego...dimittis...te...amare... I love you." Sheratan. His reason for existing. She had released him. He had forgotten everything. All of his memories. Her. In the distance, someone screaming,

"Wake up! Help her!"

Time resumed and he was slammed back into the present. Back to the same scene. The same, but different. Everything and everyone around him was moving at a pace as if under water. Lilian still cried next to him, calling out Sheratan's name. The Magnetars still sliced through endless waves of advancing demons. And Shera... his eyes dropped to her, lay there, expecting her fate. Fearless. The demon lurking over, was preparing to drive its spear through her. Rage, love, fury hit his chest like lightning and spread through his veins. His body convulsed with it. He would *not* lose her again. A power beyond words radiated from his body as he took a step forward, through the wall, as if passing through water.

Shera waited for the spear to break her skin at any moment. Knowing the demon was raising it above his head, she felt the movement of its body as the spear began its descent. Out of nowhere, the clear sound of metal rang through the air. Reverberating off everything around them. Like a tunning fork. Shera's eyes shot open to a sight she did not expect to see. Cas. He leaned over her, on one knee, his sword holding back the forked end of the demon's spear, just above her chest. She drew in a breath. "Castor." Not daring to believe it. In Cas' eyes were the memories that she had seen thousands of times. Behind them burned a fire that she never could have imagined. His body was shaking while he looked back up at the demon with pure hatred. As he stood, beams of light covered his body in piece after piece of armor. Light and strength pulsated off him. Screaming, he swung his sword once and what was left of the demon flew so far that it re-entered the mist. A shriek from Nyx was enough to stop her advancing army in their tracks. Turning around and dropping to his knees, Cas lifted Shera up to hers and wrapped his arms around her. "Cas," she whispered in his ear, placing her hand on the back of his head and burying her fingers in his hair. Pulling back and taking her face in his hands he put his mouth desperately on hers, pulling her body into his with all his strength. Time, armies, centuries faded away. Nothing existed but this moment. Just two energies, combining into one. A passionate exchange of breath between two parts of one soul, formed at the beginning of all things. Together, their minds traveled through the stars, so quickly the stars became mere streaks of blurry light. As they melted into each other a whirlwind sprung to life around them. Two glowing lights, united, in the eye of a tornado. The light grew brighter as the whirlwind took the shape of a sphere and pushed outward, expanding violently, lifting Cas and Shera off the ground, still locked in their embrace. Everyone, including their companions, watched in wonder while the nearly blinding, deafening, furious white sun spun almost out of control before coming to an abrupt stop. Then, the whirlwind evaporated, like steam into thin air and the sphere gave way to an awe-inspiring sight.

A final Magnetar. One to dwarf the others. Translucent and gleaming like the diamond armor, greenish-blue light pulsing throughout its body and blazing in its eyes. In their depths a culmination of suffering lending to the fierce power of defiant love and vengeance. Eyes that were laser focused on Nyx. Another shriek escaped from the blackness, and the army, once again, advanced. Only this time, Nyx followed.

A huge, pale, winged woman. The same

lifeless flame that burns within her demons flickering in her eyes. Her face, both beautiful and terrible, and body were covered by a black veil that billowed behind her, at length becoming the mist itself. Out of it reached shadows, arms, a sea of drowning souls crying out, pleading for help. Screams of terror erupted from the remaining humans on the ground and behind the wall. Those who hadn't already hidden began cowering or running for shelter. Cas and Shera strode forward, light cascading off them and filling the sky with seeming sunlight. Nyx turned her head slightly to shield herself from it, then let out another shriek before hurtling herself at Cas and Shera. They slammed into her, knocking her backward and into the building across the street. She disappeared for an instant in an explosion of brick and dust, mingled with the ever-moving black mist, but shot toward them again almost immediately. Hitting them square in the chest, causing them to stumble back, she rose toward the sky then quickly descended, wielding a spear. Allowing the tip of the spear to embed in their shield, they pulled it toward them and drove their sword skyward, narrowly missing Nyx as she flung herself over and landed behind them. Pulling on her end of the spear, she yanked the shield from their grasp then swung it around her body like a hammer back toward them. Kneeling to one knee, they held the sword up as it passed over their heads, cutting the edge of the spear off and allowing the shield to fall back to them. Nyx aimed the broken end at them and hurled it toward their neck. Taking a step back, they held the sword in front of them as if in salute, slicing the spear in two lengthwise, then spun their body around, launching the shield in Nyx's direction. She vanished, leaving only a breath of mist in her wake, then re-appeared directly behind them, her face close enough that they felt her breath on their neck. They started to turn, her left hand reached up, grabbing their throat, murderous rage in her expression. Before Cas and Shera had time to react, she screamed and withdrew her hand as though she'd been bitten. Shrinking backward, she gripped her wounded limb and held it up. Part of her hand was missing. It looked as though her fingers had disintegrated.

Around them, the demons that had been fighting their companions froze. The expression of rage on Nyx's face had been entirely replaced by fear. Cas and Shera looked around at their friends. She had touched them. Glancing down at their hands, they struggled to understand what had just happened. In their forearms they could see the light pulsing through. Radiating off them. There was no skin, no flesh and bone. They were energy, pure energy, almost like a forcefield. A field so strong that no shadow could pass through, not even Nyx. The light inside them was strong enough to destroy her. Suddenly, it all made sense. Why Zeus was afraid of them, why he separated them, why Nyx had waited until now to come there. Cas had become a chink in the armor when his light went dormant. But together, there was nowhere the light couldn't touch. There was nowhere for her to hide. Cas and Shera dropped their weapons and raised their eyes to Nyx. There was no need for words, their friends were of the same mind. They knew, they all knew. Dropping their weapons, as well, they moved toward Cas and Shera. Nyx looked frantically at all of them, backing up quickly toward the safety of the mist behind her. Creating a circle around Cas and Shera, the Magnetar focused their attention on Nyx and her army. Beneath them, the ground began to shake. Never before had silence been so loud. A spark, followed by a light that shone bright enough to see it from space. The field around them grew rapidly and contracted slightly, as though it were breathing, pushing outward with each breath. Swallowing all demons and shadows alike. Eradicating them in silence and light. Nyx had turned and flown at full speed into her mist, trying to call her children to her, since they were her army's generals they were closest to the mist, but they were not fast enough to escape. One by one they disappeared; their screams drowned out by the sound of nothing. Finally, when her army had been devoured and she alone was at risk, the mist vanished, with one final shriek of hatred.

All at once, the light dimmed, and the sound of the world returned. The Magnetar were no more. In their place stood a dazed group of ancient friends who, finally, understood their own existence. For a long while, nobody said anything. Nobody knew what to say. Shera's eyes met Cas' and she took his extended hand. He pulled her toward him and gently ran his thumb down her jawline. Seeing an echo of remorse on his face, she placed her hand over his cheek. "No regrets," she whispered. "You came back to me."

"I don't think I ever really left you," he said, struggling to hold back his emotion.

Finally, the circle enclosed around Cas and Shera. Sadal took Cas' arm, "I'm glad you're back, my friend."

Cas pulled him in for a hug. "Thank you for telling me to wake up."

They embraced in turn, all in slight disbelief that the ordeal was over. None of them had expected to survive the night, let alone for the events to turn as they had. The light wall was gone and people began emerging from the buildings, trying to come to grips with what they'd witnessed. A few of them had come to the aid of the soldier who had been grabbed by a demon at the beginning. He was clearly coming back to reality, but his road to recovery would be long. Nobody approached their group, they just watched in curiosity, some took pictures or pointed and whispered.

"So," Les began, posing the obvious question, "is it over?"

"I'm pretty sure she's gone, yes," Maia responded.

"I mean..." Les started.

"He means with us," Shera finished for him.

"There's no way he shows his face now," Cas fumed. "Not now."

Sadal looked at Cas and gestured to Shera. "She should be dead. That wound healed right in front of us when you merged. Even if he did show his face, there's not a damn thing he could do. Not knowing what we know now."

"So, it *is* over," Resha said.

Shera wrapped her arms around Cas. She had never held anything so tightly, in any lifetime. Her heart was bursting, but the emotion was too much for her body to contain. She shook, weeping into his neck, his arms locking around her like a vice. Relief and hope ignited among the group as they both laughed and cried at the end of their misery.

"Dad?" Lilian had appeared and was standing

a few feet away from them. Both he and Shera looked up and held their arms out to her. She threw herself into the embrace.

"I'm sorry, Baby." Cas kissed her on the forehead.

Lilian just shook her head. "You remembered." She looked at Shera who grabbed the back of her head and put their foreheads together.

Lilian turned toward the rest of the group. "Alison and Michael?"

"They're alright," Mina assured her. "They're home."

Lilian let out a sigh of relief. "You know, I think the bar is still open in there." She pointed to the building. "I'm just saying.... if anyone deserves a drink."

"Ahh.. that's a brilliant fucking idea, right there," Brach blurted out.

Cas and Shera laughed. He pulled her closer and put his lips in her hair. "I'm never letting you go," he whispered. She closed her eyes for a moment, taking it all in. The night, her friends, the battle, and her soul, here beside her, finally complete.

She opened her eyes to see Lilian beaming at them. Smiling back at her, she gestured toward the building's entrance. "Lead the way."

CHAPTER 37

Cas saw something gleaming out of the corner of his eye. Bending down to pick it up he thought it might be glass, then noticed it was actually a crystal, gleaming in the sunlight. *Figures,* he thought, *surrounded by magic.* Tossing it back to the ground he looked back up at the temple. The crew was just about finished. The grounds had been cleared and the rooms refurbished and expanded to be suites for two. The plumbing alone had been a nightmare. Plus, the courtyard was set up for proper training now and Porri had more than a fire to cook with. Grinning slightly, he found himself looking forward to the excursions here. His smile widened when he saw Shera emerge from the entrance and make her way towards him. "What do you think?"

"Show off," she teased, gaining a chuckle from him. "I think it's perfect. Couple times a year, nice and private. Maybe we can manage to stay out of the news."

"That's a stretch, Brach's eating that shit up."

Shera laughed, "Of course he is. He thinks he's Aquaman."

"Oh he'll take as many free drinks as he can get," Cas joked. There was silence for a moment. "You honestly believe she's coming back, don't you?"

"I do," Shera said seriously. "When I close my eyes.... when I see her... we took her children, Cas. Not just her army, her children. This isn't an invasion anymore, it's revenge."

"Well," he said, "If you're right, she's coming back with a much bigger army."

She leaned into him then reached over to pull his chin toward her. Locking eyes with him, she put her hand on his cheek. "Maybe we should build our own army, then. Another generation of stars. You know... just in case."

Putting his arm around her waist, he pulled her in tightly and kissed her, feeling time slip away again. "I'll fall on that grenade," he whispered.

Smiling up at him she placed her hand on his cheek. "My eternity," she whispered back, diving into his eyes, feeling the unmeasurable depths of love between them. Taking his hand, they walked toward the temple.

www.ingramcontent.com/pod-product-compliance
Lightning Source LLC
LaVergne TN
LVHW010315070526
838199LV00065B/5570